Joan Shaw

THE UNCLE
&
Other Stories

Cadmus Editions

The Uncle & Other Stories *Copyright ©1983 by Joan Shaw*
Cover illustration by Norman Rockwell copyright ©1937 & 1983
by The Curtis Publishing Company. Reprinted from The Saturday
Evening Post

All rights reserved
Printed in the United States of America

First published in 1983 by:
Cadmus Editions
Box 4725
Santa Barbara
California 93103

Acknowledgements: The short stories appeared in the following periodicals: Mademoiselle, Sibyl-Child, Snapdragon *and* Western Humanities Review.

The publication of The Uncle & Other Stories *was made possible in part by a grant from the Utah Arts Council.*

Shaw, Joan, 1930–
LCN 82-70936
ISBN 0-932274-31-5 (trade edition)
ISBN 0-932274-32-3 (signed edition)

For Alan

The writing and publication of this book were made possible in part by grants from the Carnegie Foundation and the Utah Arts Council. I feel a deep sense of gratitude to both.

THE UNCLE

THE UNCLE

I

I can hardly wait to grow up, to stare at him icily, to kill him with a look, to suffocate him with a pillow, to throw him down two flights of steps. Here, in front of the dresser mirror, I bunch my light brown hair around my ears as though it were cut short like a grown-up's. I stare icily, I frown, I kill myself with a look. I remain the same—eleven years old, minus a mother and father, a potential problem, a possible encumbrance, dull and uninteresting at that, and on top of everything, small for my age, not like Bette Davis, not like Carole Lombard. Would Charles Boyer pursue me? Would he whisper French obscenities in my ear?

* * *

What was I thinking of? I'm grown up now and long married and have a daughter of my own. All that happened long ago, what I was thinking of, what I was becoming again. I had been eleven years old, standing in front of a dresser mirror in a third-floor bedroom in a big, old house in Philadelphia. Can't you see it? Can't you just see it?

The bed is behind me—a single four-poster, with the posts carved in evenly spaced rings all the way up and down and made of a lightish wood, birch perhaps, or ash. I remember clearly a certain night. I had lain in that bed for a long time, wide awake after hearing something, something like a footstep, a whisper of a sound brushing over the carpet. And then I heard the clock strike one-thirty. The picture slips in and out of focus, the picture of me lying straight and stiff in the bed, my legs close together, covered completely by a light blanket like a corpse except for my face—a marble thing of indefinite features turned toward the bedroom door.

I become her again—an eleven-year-old girl, lying in that four-poster bed, watching the light of the pale moon filtering through the trees in the side yard and into the dormer windows on the east side of the room. I imagine the grass in shadow sweeping out before the trees below those windows and the black and cream Packard parked under the largest tree—a massive oak, planted the same year that the house was built.

I am eleven years old and I dream of myself as a languid lady of thirty or thirty-five dressed in gray silk, walking slowly in the moonlight toward the black and cream Packard while the groping shadows of the limbs and leaves of the trees move delicately back and forth over the sheer curtains covering the window glass before my sleeping eyes.

* * *

Suddenly it becomes dark and very cold. I had been asleep and dreaming of being grown up, but now I'm awake and eleven years old, startled by a sound, a footstep on the floor, and my heart leaps and pounds beneath my ribs. The night sky shows light gray through the windows and I know that someone is in my room. I keep my eyes slitted as though in sleep, with my head toward the door while the footsteps move slowly and softly across the thin carpet, whispering over the faded flowers, and then I see clearly through my eyelashes in the half-dark—I see who it is.

I would not have been uneasy at all then, but for the furtive way he walked toward me, but for the tight, electric feel of the air in the room, the peculiar way in which he pulled heavily at every breath and the fact that it was clearly the middle of the night, a period when we all should have been in the beds assigned to us.

Ah, but the dead of night—that's the time for romance. Like a warm burst of something hot and wet inside me, the picture became clear (I forget at what instant, at what hour, at what year). What better time is there for the tender affair that must not be crushed by the insensitive but kept rather like a soft, secret thing, hidden behind that dark, protective curtain? He was a man, after all, and I was a girl of eleven. What's more he was married to, of all people, my mother's sister. In point of fact, he was my uncle. There were many people who would not understand—hundreds perhaps, thousands, who would pervert the passion he felt for me into something pedestrian, perhaps low, even ugly. That of course was not the case.

I sigh and pretend to roll over in my sleep, turning my back toward him. I can feel the thin white batiste of my nightgown stretching tight across my shoulders, I can feel my heart beating against it. My bed creaks as he sits on its edge and leans toward me. His breath smells of stale cigar and peppermint and his skin of Bond Street's Lavender. My aunt is away in Baltimore.

* * *

My uncle—the urbane Lover of Walnut Hill Avenue, my surrogate father. His pockets jingle with loose change, he takes me to the store in his customized car, he leads me beside the still waters of the Delaware River at high tide when the smell from its depths is not so apparent, my cup truly runs over. He would do anything for me, anything. What do I want? He will rush right out and get it—one day when my aunt is again in Baltimore—something I'd like that is not too conspicuous, something consumable, a package of cookies, a chocolate bar, or a trip somewhere, a short trip. Where do I want to go? To Washington's Crossing to look at the bridge? To the movies to see Charles Boyer?

Le Boyer is his idol, he suffers as his idol suffers, he broods, his smoldering eyes regard me in my eleven-year-old bedroom; who can possibly understand how a man of his particular refinement suffers? Who would dare to laugh aloud at this spectacle acted out on the third floor of a dignified house on a residential street in Philadelphia in the Spring of 1941?

Ma petite cherie, ma petite Anna, he whispers hoarsely, pressing me back over his arm, his mouth close to my ear, murmuring things over and over that I can't understand but which appear to excite him unbearably. He truly loves me, he tells me in English, all of me—do I understand?—my little legs, he loves them, my round belly, my tiny tits, my dear little cunt.

His voice spins into my ears, the words spead out, they fill the room, they press heavily against the walls, they rub all over me, they concentrate hotly on my clitoris. This is something I had never seen in the movies.

I am filled with something—let us see what it could be: Desire? Confusion? Embarrassment? Even in my eleven-year-old sexual fantasies, tame and uninformed as they are, I make myself grown up and curvaceous with a bosom decorating my front that is at least worthy of the name. My face burns as hotly as what I just learned was my cunt, covered as it is with my uncle's sweaty and beringed hand. *Ah, cherie enfante, enfante cherie,* et cetera et cetera.

I am rigid with the incongruity of the situation. Stupid as I am at eleven, my memory tapes are nevertheless filled with miscellaneous information, randomly inputted at various times since I was able to think: I have done something terribly wrong.

Can I continue to live in this house after what happened, to sleep on these clean sheets, read my unaberrant books, and dream the clean, eleven-year-old dreams I'm supposed to dream in this third-floor bedroom whose windows look in three directions, affording a view the entire length and breadth of almost my entire world? Must I take upon myself the task of finding yet another home and leave this gentle, rocking ark, the entire lower half of me newly awakened to its special vocation, its vulgar place in the world, its shameful needs, its engrossing vulnerability?

* * *

The picture becomes clearer and clearer. It's 1941 in Philadelphia, and I am newly and throroughly orphaned. A few days before New Year's Day just past I came to live in this house. I had one suitcase and a box of clothes with me, my long-skirted doll, two photo albums, and some of my mother's books. My visit is to be a long one, and if things work out my aunt tells me, for all of my life perhaps. I had hoped fervently that things would work out.

This house belongs to Mrs. Loop, a short, round woman, and her crippled sister, Alice—both cousins to my uncle. My aunt and uncle have an apartment in the second floor back; I have a small room on the third floor, in the tower part of the house. My room used to be the maid's room, in the days when people on this street had maids, and is reached by a set of narrow steps coming off the main staircase in front of the house.

For my uncle to get to my room, he has either to go through his crippled cousin's bedroom or to go all the way down the back stairs, into the front hall, and up the main staircase. The main staircase has a pink marble newel post at the bottom from which extends upward a fruitwood banister. Heaven forbid that someone should accidentally fall down the steps, my mother said to me once long ago, and hit his head on that marble newel post. It would be the end of him.

* * *

I sit at the east dormer window in that childhood bedroom and look down at my uncle's car parked beneath the oak tree. The car is a 1937 Packard Super Eight, rebuilt and customized by one of the salesmen at Mrs. Loop's lumber yard where my uncle works as the floor manager. The early morning sun glints off the black fenders, off the cream hood and brilliant chrome. The car bristles with four rear-view mirrors. A winged Victory is perched on the radiator cap. The horn plays "Reveille" from two chrome bugles located beneath the headlights. My uncle has often blown the horn for me, leaning into the driver's window with his cigar clenched between his teeth, looking back at me through his blue, slightly protuberant eyes.

My uncle is walking to the car now. I see him emerge from the front door, the top of his dark-haired, squarish head first, then the rest of him. He has a jacket hanging over one arm, a cigar in his free hand. He's wearing a white shirt with the sleeves hitched up by dark green garters just below his elbows. He puts his cigar between his teeth when he reaches the car, leans back, bending one knee, and surveys the front and sides. Then he opens the driver's door and gets in.

The car roars its voice twice into the silence of the yard without moving, my uncle invisible, swallowed up inside its elegant, cream plush stomach. Then it rolls slowly and silently to the two brick-paved ribbons of the driveway, and from there out of sight and away to Loop's Lumber Yard somewhere outside South Philadelphia.

* * *

My uncle is a short man, shorter by perhaps a half-inch than my mother's sister, Aunt Lila, who is not very tall herself. His hands are thin, with squared-off fingernails, and he wears a heavy silver ring set with an onyx on his right ring finger. His dark hair is thick and brushed back in waves away from his face.

Aunt Lila said when I came to this house that if I felt so inclined I should come to her with all my problems. She covered my hand with her own, smooth and plump, and smiled at me the way she does so often—distantly, sliding her eyes away from mine at the same time as though hearing a sound somewhere to which she was giving some sort of vague attention. Perhaps she was wondering if she could love me—like her very own daughter perhaps, like the child she never had. Perhaps she was wondering if I would be worthy of that kind of love, and if I would love her back. Or perhaps she was wondering if, in taking me in, she hadn't made a mistake.

She also said to me at that time—as though an afterthought, as though to omit it were to slight him in some way, to injure some modicum of pride hidden deep down inside him, and she said it just a little testily, or perhaps a little drily, a little whimsically—that I should look upon my uncle as a father.

* * *

I look back at that time, at the house that seems as the years go by to glisten more and more with unreachable beauty. I see the tall trees in the side yard with smaller ones beneath. I see, growing close against the house, a row of old lilac, an early variety, blooming the first part of April and trimmed back closely each year so that they might not block the brick walk traveling up from the street to the front door. Voices come back to me then: the lilacs are due for their trimming, I hear Mrs. Loop say to my uncle. My uncle himself is against it. Everyone uses the driveway as a walk anyway, I hear him say back to her. In spots where the lilac is especially lush—close by the old septic tank, for instance—there are worn spots on the grass from years of detouring around the overgrown bushes. She would be better off reseeding these spots, he says, and giving the walk over entirely to the lilacs.

Mrs. Loop is always making herself and other people a lot of unnecessary work, he goes on, like the picket fence, for instance, and the locks he just put on the doors of the three empty garages.

Good locks make good sense, says Mrs. Loop. And besides, she adds, the garages are full of tools as he very well knows.

* * *

The voices echo down the halls of my mind. They sound clear and jewel-like in that persistent scene in which my tower bedroom appears like a cameo, the four-poster bed in delicate relief. My eleven-year-old skin feels crawly with cold as I lie on that bed under my light blanket. Goose bumps are spreading like measles all over my arms and legs and up my back. There is only a faint grayness showing against the black wall in my room where the windows look over the side yard. He has been gone for some time, gone back to his room in the second floor back, and I wonder if the sun will ever again show its face to me from behind the trees.

How can I look at him again, le Boyer, I wonder? How did I act? What did I say? What exactly does he think of me? Has he lost all respect?

I think and think, reliving that night, structuring and restructuring everything. I was just a child you see; I am that child now, lying under a picture of Jesus which hangs at the head of my bed. His eyes are painted so that they follow me around the room. Wherever I am, when I look at him, Jesus looks back. From my place in life now, layered over by decades of passing years, I look at the picture of Jesus and he looks out of the frame at me. My legs are cold with the memory, goose bumps climb up my back. At the same time my face is flushed, burning hot. It must be fiery red. How can I look at le Boyer again, I think to myself, how can I look at any of them?

Mrs. Loop told me once that Jesus could see everything, that he kept tabs on us all. And although I was sure what she said was a lie, I was afraid to think such thoughts out loud for fear she might possibly have been telling the truth. Mrs. Loop took me with her to mass every Sunday at Saint Thomas's Episcopal Church, since she accepted without being asked the responsibility of my religious education, and she gave me the picture of Jesus.

I lie under the picture, while Jesus and I look at the gray squares of night on the east wall of the tower. Or perhaps while I look at the windows he is looking straight down at my head, or perhaps he is looking at the door, at my uncle walking slowly and softly in his carpet slippers toward my bed.

The occasion of course is that midnight assignation which I will long remember and to which all the affectionate playfulness that went on between us during the weeks and months before so surely had led. Why is it such a surprise to me then that my uncle is now in my bedroom?

My uncle has no shirt on. A dark smudge shows up in the half-light which I take to be chest hair—a roundish spot of dark, there on the upper part of his chest. His silver ring with the black stone winks in the room in front of him.

I wonder as he walks toward me if he will look up at the picture of Jesus and if Jesus will look back at him. I wonder if Jesus will see him hold me tightly in bed, his hand under my nightgown, my aunt gone to Baltimore with Mrs. Loop, my bedroom door not bolted from the inside because there might be a fire, but closed tightly now so we wouldn't wake Alice.

My eleven-year-old eyes feel extraordinarily wide in my head, and they burn as though I were unable to blink. I am unable to scream either; that is, I scream and scream and there is no sound because my mouth is shut tight against his, my teeth clenched together against his slippery, persistent tongue. I am filled with anxiety for fear he may think by my behavior that I don't like him and become angry with me, while at the same time I burn with embarrassment for fear he may, by some action on my part, some sound, some movement, see me as a consenting female to this kind of incest, an eleven-year-old pervert, nothing less than that.

Ah, my dear uncle, I have dreamed again and again of killing you. Initiation rites for a girl of eleven—was that it?—and at least two years too early, according to Mrs. Donaghy, the foster mother I acquired soon after. Yes it would happen, she said to me—an underripe thirteen-year-old—in some alley behind the high school, by some pimply-faced kid on the basketball team, most likely a Wop, just like with every piece of trash to whose sex and age group I had the misfortune and recalcitrance to belong; or it would happen, my mother told me before she died, if I ever accepted a ride from a Stranger, or looked at any of the Sailors in the park, or talked to the Old Man who lived in the Mansion House up the street from where we lived in Hudders Wharf.

Neither one of these mothers ever mentioned the Uncle.

* * *

Ah yes, you will get yours, my handsome uncle. I have arranged it over and over. Remember it during your dizzying plunge down the front staircase, think about it as your neat, dapper head connects with that marble newel post, ah—the sickening *thunk*, the protruding eyeballs with blood welling up out of each one, the leg twisted backward, horrors!

Did you think about the consequences, you unqualified bastard, after leaving my room and groping back to the head of the stairs in the darkness? Did you ever dream what I would do to you? What did you think when you caught your foot in the little flap of carpet right before the railing, the little flap that like a magician, I lifted so very slightly, so very invitingly, from my place on my bed? Ah, my dear uncle, I have killed you again and again, in all of your guises, I have seen through all of your masks, I have ripped them from you with unbelievable savagery.

My uncle's bedroom slippers were too big for his small feet and that could be what tripped him so beautifully. Alice had given them to her cousin for his last birthday. Naturally he slid along with them instead of picking them up, and of course he was trying to be very quiet and also he was a little drunk, a little dizzy with his great conquest which turned out to be such an easy one. I was such a young thing, so pure. How much purer can you get than eleven years old without even any pubic hair?

There was some kind of innocence surrounding me, you see, some touching kind of vulnerability into which my uncle fell as though drowning. We must understand this kind of man. We must forgive him, offer him counseling, understanding, medication. He couldn't help himself—love is a disease after all. There should be a vaccine developed for it, some kind of prevention, since there is no cure. He was helpless in the face of my charms, my little legs, for instance, and after all, did I not entice him nymphet that I was? Could I not see what I was doing to him on those trips to Washington's Crossing to look at the bridge, on those walks to the corner drugstore for cookies and root beer? How long can a man stand to be excited by the voluptuousness of a round-bellied eleven-year-old? Did I not sit on his lap just the Sunday before? How long can a man hold up under such provocation?

The scenes from my Walnut Hill Avenue Hollywood dreams recur and recur: *Ma cherie, ma cherie*—my head is bent back under le Boyer's mouth. My gray silk dress rustles and my satin pumps fall off my feet. Could this be my uncle in some disguise? He loves me, all of me, do I understand? My little legs, my dear little cunt . . . the words reverberate against the walls of my head; they echo down the corridors of all my years. I laugh and laugh at it all.

They look so ridiculous, the grown-up men—by turn humble and proud, formal and casual, arranging important papers on their desks, folding back the pages on their citation books and drawing the pen from its place in the flap, riding the palomino into the arena, talking earnestly behind the lectern, brandishing the chalk at the blackboard, walking by twos and threes into the boardrooms. What goes on under the skin of their heads?

See the high dormer windows up there on the third floor of the tower—there on the east side of the house? They were mine for a little while. The white ninon curtains that cover the glass inside move delicately in the breeze generated by the spring flowers, by the leafing trees, by my uncle's recently requited love. I show people these windows, a laugh barely suppressed under my ribs. It was all so funny, I say to them; why do I give any of it a single thought?

* * *

Behind the curtains I show them is my bedroom and above my bed hangs an eight-by-ten picture of Jesus whose eyes are painted so that they follow my own no matter from which side of the room I look at them—a fiendish gift from my catechist, Mrs. Loop. I have even gone far to the side of the picture and still those eyes looked back at me.

On the other hand, my uncle never looked at the picture of Jesus. If my uncle never looked at Jesus, Jesus never looked at him. If Jesus didn't look at my uncle, perhaps he didn't see what went on. If he didn't see it, perhaps it didn't happen, perhaps it was a dream I had. I have often had dreams that I believed for a long time were not dreams at all, but reality. People often have very vivid dreams, so vivid that it takes days, years, for them to get over that particular kind of reality and back into the dream of life.

Really, it couldn't have happened. To tell you the truth, it didn't happen.

In fact, it was something I made up.

To think that an uncle would do such a thing, Anna, for shame; why do you want to get your uncle in trouble? Where do you get such ideas anyway?

* * *

My uncle has left me alone in my bedroom and has closed the door behind him. I'm startled almost immediately by the sudden grunt of surprise at the head of the steps right outside my room. I wince at the scraping of fingernails against the wall as my uncle falls down the first flight of stairs, rolling head over heels. I wince at the sound as he hits the first landing. Down he goes now, down the other flight, tumbling over and over, knocking against the banister, against the wall. And then I hear the final, the sickening *thunk,* as his handsome head hits the pink marble newel post.

And then—the ominous quiet.

What have I done? I lie straight and stiff under my blanket in the dark room, and wait for something to happen.

There is no one else home but Alice. Did she hear the sounds as I did while my uncle tumbled down on his totally unexpected trip past the hallway leading to her bedroom? Will she slip heavily out of her bed, pull herself with her arms across the smooth linoleum floor of her room, turn on the hall light, and slide down the steps, one by one, on her wide calloused bottom, to find him there, one arm lying across her empty wheelchair? Will she scream for little Anna?

Alice's loose slightly moist mouth hangs open, terror-stricken. Her watery blond hair glints under the hall light as she sits there on the fifth step from the bottom.

Anna! she screams.

Aaaaannnnaaaa! Aaaaaaannnnnaaaaaa!

* * *

But I am not in my bed, nor even in my room. It's early afternoon, my uncle is out painting the new picket fence, and I am in the downstairs bathroom pulling down my white cotton knit panties. I've been sitting in the bathroom on the side of Mrs. Loop's tub since right after lunch, holding her mirror in my hand. Now, with my panties off and lying in a heap on the pink chenille cover of the toilet, I've brought myself to look, I must look, because my mother once told me that the snatches of little girls who allowed themselves to be touched by men very often turn . . .

. . . black.

II

A long, loud, hollow wail, a horn moaning for the dead, a cow lamenting for her lost calf, Alice yelling at the foot of the main staircase. I lie trembling in my four-poster bed in that Philadelphia house in 1941, my heart leaping and pounding against my ribs, wide awake now, thanks to the most effective of all alarm clocks: Alice yelling at the foot of the steps for her sister in the kitchen—Baarbaraaaa, Baarbaraaaa—the call echoing up the stairwell and through my bedroom door.

It has been four weeks now since my uncle visited me here in my bedroom. Not a word since has he uttered to me about it; the walks to the drugstore go on as before, the requests for turpentine and wiping cloths as he paints the new picket fence have no sultry undertones. He only looks at me.

In the side yard, in the dining room, drying the dishes in the kitchen, sitting across from him at the drugstore lunch table, I lift up my eyes to look around and, like those of Jesus in my room, his eyes lock with mine. À la Boyer, they brood and smolder—who could possibly understand how a man of his particular refinement suffers?

I have stopped looking up altogether when he is anywhere within walking distance. The dishes I'm drying, the table in front of me, the ground below my feet, they all become intensely interesting at those times.

When will he come again? Do I dare to bolt my bedroom door? I listen to the yells of Alice and wonder. Meanwhile her predicament has become clear to me: for the second time this week Mrs. Loop has moved Alice's wheelchair into the dining room in the process of vacuuming the front hall and has failed to put it back. Alice would prefer not to pull herself all the way into the dining room to retrieve it, drag it back to the steps, set the brake, and climb back up the stairs to the proper height for lifting her strange bulk into it.

Where is Mrs. Loop? Bacon is obviously frying in the kitchen; the aroma is rippling its way up the staircase, piggy-backing the yells of

Alice. I jump up finally, throw off my nightgown and pull on my light blue dress from yesterday and a pair of cotton panties from my dresser drawer. I'll run down the steps and get the wheelchair and bring it back to Alice, anything to stop that hoarse cry, that bawl, that indictment of Creation.

But as my bare feet reach the second landing, scruffy white sandals clutched in my right hand, Mrs. Loop materializes, trundling the wheelchair in from the dining room. Her frizzy red hair glints and sparkles in the sunshine coming through the big crescent of glass at the top of the front door. Murmurs of apology and acquittal pass between the two sisters, Alice lifts herself into the wheelchair under her sister's watchful eyeglasses, and Mrs. Loop steers her out to the kitchen.

Unseen, unnoticed, I follow them, follow the pied-piper smell of frying bacon lying lightly on the early Saturday morning air in that big, towering house that I had hoped at one time would be my permanent home. I follow them, looking intently all the while at the carpet under my feet.

* * *

Bacon cracks and pops in the frying pan—a black and businesslike affair sitting fourteen inches across on the enormous eight-burner gas range which dominates the west wall of the kitchen. I'm the second one to the table this morning. Alice is already there stirring her coffee, smiling at me with her loose, moist smile. My uncle is out washing and waxing his car and will eat later. Today is Saturday, hence the leisurely breakfast cooked by Mrs. Loop, who all week long runs her late husband's lumber yard from a cavernous office situated on the second floor of the lumber yard showroom. Mrs. Loop, Aunt Lila, and I are going today with my uncle to Wannamaker's to buy gifts for Alice's birthday tomorrow.

I try not to look at Alice eating her eggs. The path from plate to mouth appears a terrible risk, guided as it is with her awkward hands. And yet not so much as a crumb litters her place at the table while I, with young and healthy hands, manage to leave a mountainous mess.

Alice has just told me that we will have our crocheting lesson right after breakfast. I watch my scrambled eggs as I eat. I don't mind learning how to crochet, but would rather that Aunt Lila, or

Mrs. Loop, or even a total stranger teach me how than Alice, and this urgent disinclination shames me.

Alice always smells like perfumed soap. She smiles her loose smile at me each time I come into a room where she is. She asks me in her hoarse voice each morning how I slept the night before. What is it that bothers me about Alice then? Is it her strange, thick torso, her thin, helpless little legs, her shapeless mouth, her throaty voice? Shame wells up to the crown of my head: to dislike a person for such despicable reasons! Is it her concern with my well-being? Is it her worry that I may not be sleeping well? Is it her terrible desire to be loved by me as she must be loved by all the women in this house? Is it her interest in everything I do, in everything I feel?

But could Alice be my only understanding friend here? Could I not let the incident with my uncle slip out during one of our crocheting lessons, after I take account of the situation between her and me and perhaps find it favorable to confess the thing?

Is there some hidden understanding of life and its amusing, playful vagaries in that strange, lumpish body? Would she understand immediately how it is with men in general and with my uncle in particular and advise me somewhat on what to do, on how to act, on which way to handle the thing so that perhaps I could eliminate the problem, or even eliminate my uncle? Yes, eliminate him and still remain a loved and loving member of this household, still retain my tower room on the third floor where I can see everything in the yard to the third and last garage, and ahead and behind to the mysterious houses stretching up and down Walnut Hill Avenue, with their elegant chimneys and pointed roofs, their washyards into which women disappear and hang clothes, showing only their hands and sometimes the tops of their heads—sheets and pillowcases, tablecloths, towels and blankets, becoming for me sails: jibs and foresails, staysails and mainsails that whistle and snap in the wind, carrying the latticework enclosures on journeys that only I can perceive while I sit on the dark needlework cushion of my dormer window—would she understand?

Would she tell me that, of course, no one in the family really likes him anyway, the gigolo, the fool, the hanger-on? Could we, Mrs. Loop, Aunt Lila, Alice, and I, become a family of widows and virgins, a community of Religious, dedicated to the Queen of Heaven, perhaps, praising her with our *Aves* in the mornings and in the nights?

Could Alice have stolen out of her bed in the dark, pulling herself with her thick, powerful arms across the linoleum of her bedroom and onto the carpet of the hall and up the narrow steps to my room and, there in the pale light coming from the small, high window in the hall of the tower in which I sleep, pulled up the flap of carpet at the head of the steps, making it just loose enough to be missed on the way up but treacherous on the way down, knowing exactly what my uncle had in mind as he walked so quietly up those steps to my bedroom that night? I structure and restructure, invent and orchestrate, change and remedy—if the bolt on my door had been shot through, if my aunt had not gone to Baltimore with Mrs. Loop, if my uncle had died instead of my mother, if he had plunged down the steps right after and crushed his head on the marble newel post . . .

Should I tell Alice? Should I speak to her now of the common predicament we find ourselves in, we two cripples, the predicament those all around us appear to admire so much—our collective life?

But could I stand up under cross-examination? And what questions would she ask me? And did I have any answers at all?—never mind whether they would be the right ones or not. Why did I let him stay in my bedroom? Why didn't I scream for Alice? What did I feel? Do I love my uncle? Do you love your dear uncle? Do you love me *ma cherie enfante?* His voice is hoarse, his hand is hot, covering as it is . . .

No, no, I cannot tell Alice.

* * *

Mrs. Loop will eat with Alice and me, she announces, and will then clean up with little Anna's help. My uncle will clean up after himself as usual. Aunt Lila seldom eats breakfast on Saturday, but rests in bed until midmorning and makes up for her fast at lunch.

Mrs. Loop lifts four slices of bacon out of the pan and turns off the gas flame. Her eggs lie perfectly round on her plate. Banks of cookbooks line the wall next to the range. Against them her frizzy, flying hair looks as though it has just received a charge of electricity and is trying desperately to recover its decorum. It glints and winks in front of the shelves in the sunlight streaming across the kitchen and onto the white wooden cupboards, across the cookbook shelves, against the wall next to the gas range. Before she leaves the range Mrs. Loop puts her plate aside and turns on the gas jet in the big oven. It must heat up for the bread and rolls, now rising in several pans on the rack high above it. The smell of yeast mingles pleasantly with the bacon and toasting bread, with the coffee and the open jar of strawberry jam in front of me. A faint whiff of gas drifts across the room as Mrs. Loop lights the oven. I look at Mrs. Loop and remember something suddenly and with a painful lurch at my insides: my mother is dead. There is a biting, spicy smell coming from somewhere . . .

* * *

The spicy smell is the mustard in the big jar on the pretzel wagon; a large, flat stick protrudes from the top. Mrs. Loop and I are on Market Street, watching the Mummers' Parade. Ranks of fat, soft pretzels, lying in rows on the open-air shelf of the wagon release their new-baked smell into the cold of the Philadelphia air. The wagon's window is propped open on my side, its bicycle wheels stand still beside me.

I hold a pretzel in a square of white oiled paper, mustard smeared generously across the top. I've bitten off both ends of the knot, those browned ends that are sprinkled the heaviest with chunky salt. Now Mrs. Loop and I lean forward to see the next string band marching down Market Street. Someone behind me sings the song they play—Oh, them golden slippers, Oh, them golden slippers. The band members are dressed in satin—green, white, and gold—the feathers and fringe flouncing with every step as they march.

It's New Year's Day. Mrs. Loop has taken me to see the Mummers' Parade while my Aunt Lila stays with my mother in the Camden County Hospital. My suitcase and box of clothes, my photo albums, my mother's books have been hastily dropped in the middle of my new room on the third floor of the house on Walnut Hill Avenue, things still not settled in properly because of additional packing to be done in the Hudders Wharf house. My mother will soon follow me to Philadelphia, they say, as soon as she is well enough to be driven the distance in my uncle's car.

The banjos and guitars, the clarinets and brilliant saxophones swing from side to side with the gait of the satin-costumed players as they march, slipping their feet along in gilded shoes. The elegantly dressed mummers follow the band, holding their arms out to spread the magenta and silver of their sleeves like sails, their feathery headdresses ruffling back in the January wind, sliding their gilded shoes back and forth across the wide street, their legs bent at the knees, crossing each other in complex patterns, bowing to the crowds of spectators on the sidewalk. The crowds applaud them; some of the people laugh and call out to those among the mummers that they know.

One of the dancers slips and slides toward my place on the sidewalk, bows with a great show of reverence, and lifts up his wind-reddened face and winks at me. His eyes are bloodshot. The strong smell of whiskey lacing his breath becomes a crucible of memories, a bridge spanning the years. . . . The kitchen table rocks as he leans against it and my teacup rattles, spilling tea all over the porcelain top. His elderly sister calls him sharply from the next room, but he has by now a firm hold on my hand and is grinning at me boozily. His sister comes to the door. "Percy, Percy," she says.

I am seventeen, seventeen.

* * *

My mother never came from the hospital in Camden to Philadelphia. And while I stuffed myself with mustard-smeared pretzels and ice cream and hot chocolate, my mother was breathing with more and more difficulty in her hospital bed during a coma into which she had fallen right after my last visit. Why do they try to spare children the facts of death? I will never forgive them. I will never forgive myself for not knowing, not saying goodbye to her. Why did they not say to me, "Look, Anna, your mother is dying. She will never come back to you, will never take you for walks again along the beach, will never warn you again of Old Men and Sailors. You will never again have someone to whom you can run and tell your most loathsome secret and expect forgiveness as if from your own personal deity. Anna, you have lost your only friend."

* * *

Mrs. Loop is talking to me in her exceptionally small voice, a voice it seems that is almost an overreaction to Alice's hoarse and throaty delivery, a voice that seems almost to be held down by force. Do you remember the Nicene Creed, Anna? she asks me. My mouth is full of toast and strawberry jam—always the glutton, as though desperate to grow a little, both up and out. I nod my head yes.

All I remember of the Nicene Creed at this particular instant are the first two words, "I believe . . ." I pray fervently that Mrs. Loop will not ask me to repeat it to her.

This is no time to be reciting creeds, Baarbaraa, bawls Alice across the table as she reaches for the jam jar.

Outside, my uncle, his cigar clenched between his teeth, is walking toward the kitchen window to turn on the faucet there which is connected to the hose. Mrs. Loop looks at his small, handsome head while she sips at her coffee thoughtfully. I must finish sharpening the shears, she says quietly to us. The shears, she adds, forking up a piece of egg to her mouth, must be extremely sharp (she is now chewing) if they are to do the job properly. Amazingly, I hear every word, for though Mrs. Loop's voice is exceptionally quiet, it's also exceptionally clear and distinct, like the edge on the blades of the slender, brilliantly sharp garden shears.

I also look at my uncle's head—and see it covered with blood. I see him strangling, the hose wound tightly around his neck. I see his blue, puffy face, I see his tongue lolling messily out of his mouth. When will he come again? Will it be after Alice's birthday, when Mrs. Loop and Aunt Lila go again to Baltimore to visit Mrs. Loop's sister, May? Do I dare bolt my bedroom door when they leave? Could I perhaps talk them into taking me to Baltimore with them?

I look at Mrs. Loop's eyes, clear and sharp and small behind her glasses, while she in turn looks at my uncle. What could it be behind those eyes? What does she think of my uncle?

* * *

I rearrange and invent; my murder mystery reading adds sophistication and polish to everything. I see him there, lying at the foot of the steps, my uncle in that awkward position, and I sigh with relief that there is now no need to beg for a trip to Baltimore or to bolt my bedroom door. He appears to be thoroughly dead.

But his eyes—there seems to be something puzzling about his eyes. They seem not to be bulging out *enough* for such a fatal injury to the head. And how could he have fallen so perfectly and hit his head so surely on that marble newel post as to cause his instant death, anyway?

How did they all feel about my uncle in this house? Did Alice love him or hate him or feel indifferent to him? Had he secretly tormented her as a little girl, out of sight of the others—she with her useless, scrawny legs and her rapidly growing body, her difficulty for so many years to speak properly, for instance, to sound her "s"? Had he laughed and called her unkind names, this little boy who obviously had been born so beautiful and had been petted and pampered no doubt by his mother, a teacher at the public school, comparing to himself Alice's already monstrous and embarrassing features with his own, delicate and fine?

It's true that my uncle rarely looks at Alice, even when speaking to her directly. That is, when answering some question of hers which he cannot possibly avoid, he never looks into her eyes, but somewhere to the left or right of her head, or at times across one of her shoulders, or at other times into her lap.

Whenever Alice presents her obligation to my uncle at Christmas or on his birthday, the gift is always in some way unsuitable; for instance, the electric fan she gave him for Christmas. Or not quite proportionate; for instance, the slippers she gave him for his birthday that were one whole size too large.

Alice knows full well the size of my uncle's shoes—how could she not?—the subject comes up at least once a week at table, brought up usually by himself: the incredible smallness and daintiness of his feet. Even I knew at once the size of my uncle's feet after I moved here.

My uncle expresses his gratitude for these obviously inappropriate offerings with no hint of surprise or chagrin. And so does the rest of the family looking on. And does Alice watch her cousin fixedly from under her lashes I wonder? And is there a smile trying to form itself around her loose, shapeless mouth? My uncle places the fan on the shelf by his platform rocker close by the window and plugs the cord into the nearby outlet so the fan is at the ready in case of the slightest need, and he shuffles along with an equanimity absolutely astounding for my often-petulant uncle in his too-large slippers.

I'm almost sure that these gifts are Alice's joke, perhaps even the whole family's joke on my unlovable and helpless uncle. Am I going too far? Am I restructuring things too much?

But her gifts to others in the family seem remarkably well thought out. For instance, the inexpensive but precious binoculars she gave me for my christening last week, so convenient for me to survey suburban Philadelphia from my tower bedroom windows that face north, east, and west. Perhaps the choice of that particular gift for me was just a happy accident, like the French cookbook she gave to her sister, Mrs. Loop, who reads the thing assiduously morning and night, and who has plied us with *poisson à la parisienne,* and *boeuf aux champignons* and *quiche Lorraine* and other dishes too numerous and confusing to remember ever since she got it and who consults the creamy buckram-covered book, her fingertips touching affectionately the *fleurs de lis* running in orderly columns down the spine, even in her rocker on the back porch, rocking in the early spring sun on Saturdays and Sundays.

Perhaps Alice's comments on Hitler's bloody tank ride through Europe, her defense of President Roosevelt in the teeth of my uncle's comments on his war-mongering, the smiling derision she heaps, forcing it heavily through her thick throat, upon Father Coughlin, are only impressive to me, an eleven-year-old, to whom the news on the radio and in the daily papers comes from another world with which I have no correspondence at all. And perhaps the respectful murmurs of interest and agreement from Mrs. Loop and the supporting remarks contributed by my Aunt Lila on the Versailles fiasco, the Munich agreement, and the Polish Corridor are merely kindnesses shown by them to Alice because of her particular condition.

But nevertheless, someone has murdered my uncle, who is lying now at the foot of the steps mysteriously very dead, for I can see blood, not only from his poor, broken skull and protruding eyes, but from his back, too—and what do we have here? A gash! A long, gaping, wide-open gash, cleanly cut at the edges, and deep, deep in his back.

Stabbed in the back.

Well.

But who did it?

Let us check over the list of suspects. It could not have been little Anna who had not nearly the strength. Nor Mrs. Loop, fastidious Mrs. Loop, who, if she chose to stab my uncle, would do so behind the garages in front of the trash cans where the mess would not so much matter, luring him there on some pretext or other, perhaps to put a lock on the tiny tool shed back there, essentially empty of valuable goods, but holding the bricks to extend the walk from the front porch across the grass to the gate in the picket fence, and therefore eligible for some substantial type of security.

Could it have been Aunt Lila, who had finally despaired, cool and distant as she might be, of his ability to grow up? Was it her own forty-fifth birthday present to him a month early—she to be in less than thirty days six years older than he was in years and twenty-six years older in common sense and intelligence, as I heard her say icily to him only last month in the privacy of their apartment on the second floor back of this house?

Could it have been Alice?

Could Alice have attacked him on the stairs, and with her powerful arms thrust the shears, closed tight with the little clip on the handle, deep into his beautifully shaped, delicate back? Could it have been because of what little Anna told her during their last crocheting lesson? Could that intelligence have suddenly brought back to her all those well-felt torments and wrongs and cruelties that must have happened long ago and thus drove her to do such a fearful thing, a thing so dangerous to herself?

And if she did, what would they do to Alice? Would they call the inspector and haul her off to jail?

III

I have been reading avidly for several months since I came here to Walnut Hill Avenue. Alice has several shelves of mystery novels among her books, my favorites up to now being Ellery Queen, Agatha Christie, and Sherlock Holmes. My Aunt Lila doesn't think Sherlock Holmes so very bad for an eleven-year-old girl to read but is more or less appalled in her cool and detached way, by the thought of her small niece shrinking and shivering in her third-floor bedroom over the violence and depravity printed in the others. So she spends much of her sewing business money on cardboard-covered editions of Nancy Drew and Tom Swift in an effort to change the direction of my literary inclinations.

And these gifts from my aunt I also read, having amassed a

two-foot-long collection on the top of my dresser—although the level of sophistication in the Drew and Swift mysteries and those in the others, of course, couldn't possibly be compared. My aunt's books I therefore dispense with quickly and linger, fascinated, over the ones I borrow from Alice's shelves.

Alice, regardless of my aunt's obvious feelings about the matter, allows me free access to her books; or rather, she ignores completely my excursions, or perhaps I should say my incursions, into her room to pilfer one or two books at a time and gorge myself in my tower room on oriental daggers, exotic poisons, ribbons of blood creeping insidiously from under closed doors, and the puzzling behavior of suspects—who number among the majority of characters populating these stories.

I would go further on this subject and say that Alice even approves of my reading, for sitting together on the back porch—I in the high-backed rocker beside Alice in her wheelchair, painfully at work on the single crochet over my left index finger—she will often question me hoarsely and intimately, as though this subject had nothing to do with anyone else in the family except the two of us sitting together at this important work, as to what I thought of the conduct of Jane Marple in some particular incident in a Christie novel which she had apparently noticed missing from the neat columns of her shelves of books like a recently extracted tooth, or how I enjoyed the opening chapter of a particularly scary Ellery Queen story, the paperback corner of which she could plainly see poking out of the pocket of my green plaid sundress.

Ah, Alice, Alice! Could I have found in you my savior, my intercessor? Could I have crawled into your lap the Morning After, moving up against your broad belly to spare your tiny legs the weight of my sixty- or seventy-pound body, and pressed my aching and guilty head against your virgin dugs, and confessed the thing to you, and cried out as though to the Blessed Virgin Mary, the Queen of Heaven, that no matter how it looked, that no matter what my uncle might say, that I was not to blame? Could I have gone that far?

And Alice, would you have believed me? Would I have believed myself? Did I ever believe such a thing at all?

Because as everyone knows, children are always to blame and the children know it too. That they are born naturally full of guilt and expect punishment for anything and everything as we all expect the rain to fall downward is evident in the way they turn around, their eyes wide with theatrical innocence, when called by an adult with even the smallest edge to her voice, and flying through their minds immediately, one overtaking and perhaps trampling the other, are memories of possible infractions of household or schoolhouse rules, sins of commission and sins of omission, excursions perhaps forbidden, shoes left recently muddy, socks forgotten under the bed, crayons left in the pockets of dirty jeans and found later in the washing machine among a load of expensive clothes dyed pink or blue or green or perhaps all three.

And as you know, children always lie, and especially girls, who learn the art much more quickly than boys; and a girl will lie for all sorts of reasons—to get an adult in trouble for instance, because that adult had perhaps denied her some privilege, like going for a ride in his cream and black Super Eight Packard up to Washington's Crossing on the Delaware River last Sunday when he could have very easily done so, the car being clean and bright after its Saturday purification and he having nothing to do on Sunday but listen on the radio to the first game of the season between the Boston Orioles and the Chicago White Sox.

And of course, there was that bolting of the bedroom door after he expressly forbade me to do so because of fire, and perhaps many other infractions of his rules, because as everyone hears at the table and around the radio in the evenings and on Sunday afternoons, my uncle is a firm believer in rigorous discipline when touching upon the behavior of girls bordering on puberty—so much more so than in the case of boys who are not nearly so vulnerable and besides, being male, mature in that respect so much later.

Ah, Alice, what would he say about me, little Anna, in his own defense? The seat on the witness stand in a rape trial for me, the victim of the rape, the questions, the insinuations—all of which we have heard about in movies starring Gregory Peck and read about in novels and in interviews written up in women's magazines—all that would be nothing to compare with it.

What would Mrs. Loop think of me, little Anna, of whose religious and therefore moral education she has taken complete control? What would Aunt Lila do to me? How would she ever know, for the rest of her life, perhaps, which one of us was telling the truth?

* * *

Married now and with a girl of my own, I look out my bedroom window and across the yard to the field dotted with aspen in the early morning sun—over two thousand miles from Philadelphia, years from the house on Walnut Hill Avenue, from my uncle, from Alice. The aspen have just opened their light green leaves. They rise delicately out of the darker green of the fingering canyon maples and tremble against the junipers far beyond them. One clump of aspen grows at the edge of the yard. The leaves tremble in the breeze. The roots reach like hands into the bare ground, the fingers holding tightly to the soil beneath, sucking up its sweetness in the warm ecstasy of sunlight.

The field stretches straight and flat to the foothills. The grass lies down in the breeze and yellow leaves from last fall skitter over it. Someone looks up from the bending grass toward the window behind which I stand unobserved. It is a child, a little girl. She grows before my eyes as she walks toward the house—an eleven-year-old, her white knit shirt lies lightly over the small, rounded buds of her breasts.

Does she know that I could easily die and leave her? I want to tell her everything I know, everything I feel. My dear one, my daughter who is myself reincarnated—you are that much like your mother—do you know what pain and perplexity is in store for you, even with me here to fight for you, perhaps to kill for you? Yes, to strangle any offender with a joy that could not possibly be contained, to tear apart anyone who dared to approach you as though to harm you?

It is spring in the Rocky Mountains. The leaves glow pale green on the trees by my bedroom window. Their groping shadows move back and forth across the curtain over the glass in the first rays of sun coming over the mountains. I stand at the window behind this sheer curtain and look out. The white geese cry; they leave the field where the sheep are grazing to search through the grass by my window. They stretch their necks out and spread their wings and lift them up and down in the warming breeze. The little girl walks quietly behind them so as not to send them running across the yard and down the hill. The soft, half-grown goslings are herded by the geese in the middle, but the smallest one falls back out of the flock. The girl walks quietly toward it, scoops it up, holds its plump body under one arm and gently rubs with her right index finger the soft down of its head and its belly, strokes the new white feathers in its tail. She is my daughter; she is her mother; she is I, myself.

Her uncle is there by the oak tree, caressing, rubbing, fondling his cream and black car, watching the girl with his blue, slightly protuberant eyes, which are nevertheless quite striking in their wide, oval openings. The irises of his eyes are very dark. He broods gloomily, he aches with desire, he feels so deeply, only he can appreciate whatever it is that he feels. Soon he will lay down the piece of cloth he is using to rub the chrome of his car and go softly and quietly after her, sliding his loose, needlepoint carpet slippers soundlessly through the grass.

But I am there behind him, slowly following him and softly, too, so as not to frighten him off. Can you see me stalking him out there like a tiger? Can you see how well I slink along, my shoulders hunched forward, my hands curved into claws, invisible to him—the poor, insensible bastard?

And then suddenly I spring upon him! I tear at his back, his thick head of hair. I have him down, all unawares, and roll him over; his pop eyes, terrified, look up at me. My God! He had thought I was dead. I had been dead for almost five months! a year! thirty-five years! I tighten my incredibly strong, vise-like fingers around his delicate throat. I squeeze and squeeze and laugh uproariously into his livid, terrified face. I exult in the death I'm creating. If I had the strength, if there were the time, if there were the possibility, I would gladly continue in this ecstasy, this orgasm, this religious absolution, forever, expiating by this act my ignominious sin, my terrible rage, my impotent fear for my daughter, for all the daughters of this earth.

I have killed him over and over—with a well-placed word like a stiletto, with a laugh that shriveled an embryonic pride. I have plotted all my life on ways to suck him dry, I have structured and restructured that night, I have murdered lovers in bed. The Fathers placed over me, the Uncles controlling my destiny, they rearrange their papers carefully on one side of their desks, their calendars are full of important names and dates, they are marked by me with his sign. They grasp uncertainly at the lectern, deflated at the reaction that had come too soon. Laughter reaches them from across the hall, they stumble, they mispronounce a word, they forget the end of the story. Will I ever lay his ghost? Will I ever punish him enough?

Who will love me, a twelve-year-old girl? Who will identify with my irritating and idiotic idiosyncrasies when I am thirteen, fourteen, fifteen? Who loves me, only me? To whom am I more important than anything else in the world? Who will forgive me all of my trespasses? Who will bathe away all of my hate?

* * *

Breakfast is over, my crocheting lesson is over, the kitchen is cleaned up, and Mrs. Loop has hurried outside, anxious to get two hours' worth of lilac clipping finished before she must hurry back in and take the ten or fifteen minutes needed for her to shower and change for our shopping trip.

Aunt Lila has had her coffee *seul* in her sewing room; my uncle has eaten his spartan breakfast of boiled egg, coffee, and toast—a habit born of weighing in each morning upon arising—and cleaned up the dishes.

I am fresh from my bath and dressed in the costume dictated to me by my aunt before I left for the bathroom: pink and white two-piece dress, made for me by my aunt only last week, pink anklets, expressly against Mrs. Loop's wishes since it's early May and still nippy at certain times of the day, white shoes, and pink sweater.

I hear Alice call to me from the back porch. I go to see what's up and she shows me that she has dropped her crochet hook in favor of knitting needles. now embarking on a tan sweater with a picture of a cocker spaniel on the back.

I am delighted and sit on the rocker beside her, careful not to brush the sides of it with my fragile costume. I gaze at the sweater pictured on the other side of the sheet of directions. I saw it in a needlework magazine I was leafing through with Alice a few weeks before and admired it energetically. It will go into my fall wardrobe, Alice tells me and, suddenly assuming what could pass for an authoritarian frown, growls to me that I must not, under any circumstances, grow any more than one size before September.

Gladly, I think, looking at the sweater. I'll cut down on my eating; I'll join my aunt in her banana and grapefruit diet; I'll exercise with her in her sewing room.

I marvel as I sit beside Alice, musing over my fall wardrobe crowned by this lovely knitted item, at her patience with me during my crocheting lessons. I marvel at this strange, lumpish woman I fear so much to touch, as though her handicap were somehow foul or contagious. No matter how many single crochets I do backward, no matter that, when she attends to her own work, allowing me to finish one row on my own, I botch the thing so beautifully that we must tear out the whole piece and start again from scratch. No matter, no matter. Alice smiles and leans over to me, arranges my fingers in the right way, starting me off again with the impossible chain ring and the first row of single crochets that must be squeezed into its tiny circumference.

My mother, I think to myself, would have long ago given up in despair, would have thrown crochet hook, crocheted piece, and ball of thread clear across the lawn in a perfect fury of impatience. And although she would hold me afterwards and perhaps even cry and ask forgiveness for her intemperate show of pure and simple rage, she would nevertheless still maintain that I was indeed a hard student, a perfect wonder to teach anything to.

And that was all right. I had always expected impatience, learning as I usually did so slowly and with such great difficulty, and in some way this impatience expiated for me the guilt of knowing I was causing someone so much trouble.

A large degree of patience, on the other hand, always created for me a great deal of uneasiness. I was always expecting the axe to finally fall, and it usually did, with a great deal of noise and unmitigated fury. I knew, I was absolutely certain, that I would some day pay for the trouble I was causing Alice.

A conspiratorial whisper jerks me around in my seat and I see Mrs. Loop beckoning me to come into the kitchen. It is time, apparently, to go get Alice's birthday gifts. Alice in her wheelchair takes great pains during this short exchange to appear deaf and dumb.

My aunt is standing in the kitchen waiting to receive me for inspection, which I never seem to pass. Mrs. Loop stands aside while Aunt Lila pulls my dress straight and runs a comb through my already tangled hair. How does my hair get tangled so quickly, I wonder despairingly, having just brushed it dry less than a half-hour before.

Aunt Lila is dressed in a pale rose crepe dress, the knife-pleated skirt brushing the tops of her calves, and she looks for all the world like England's Queen Mary. Mrs. Loop is dressed in a brown dress, looking for all the world like Mrs. Loop and no one else—looking like Mrs. Loop on her way to work or on her way to town or to the doctor's or dentist's.

Mrs. Loop worries that my legs will get cold. Aunt Lila tells her the thermometer on the front porch is registering at this particular minute seventy-five degrees Farenheit. Mrs. Loop informs her that air in the Spring is entirely different from the air in the Summer and that temperature readings mean little when all is said and done. That is, seventy-five degrees in the summer is an entirely different proposition compared with seventy-five degrees in the spring.

Aunt Lila ignores this climatic treatise, having found close to my lower scalp a large wad of tangled hair and is engrossed with trying to untangle it without too much pain on her niece's part—a hopeless attempt, as it turns out. She talks to me in defense of the excruciating pain she's inflicting—of the importance of combing my hair *all the way through*, rather than merely brushing over the top.

Outside, my uncle is peevishly waiting for us in his cream and black plaything, finally being obliged to honk the horn; that is, he is obliged to blow "Reveille". Mrs. Loop makes a sound of annoyance with her mouth. Never mind, my aunt tells her— carrying a good bit of my hair across the room to the wastecan—it could be "Taps". Yes, she says, walking back with the brush in her hand, it could be "Taps".

For me, it *is* "Taps", and the bugle is playing it mournfully. Wishfully thinking, I can hear it quite plainly through the pain of torn-out hair and perhaps, for all I know, a piece of missing scalp. The sound of the tune echoes through the low hills and tall trees of Oakwood Cemetery. My uncle, having spent one-sixth of a year in the army in late 1917, and having died through some fortuitous circumstance or other just the other day, is being buried with all the trappings of a *bona fide* veteran. Close to the grave site stand my aunt and Mrs. Loop. Beside them is Alice in her wheelchair. Mrs. Loop rests her right hand on Alice's shoulder. All of their eyes are red with weeping while their faces, in contrast, are drained of color. Soon they will each drop clods of dirt on the casket as it is lowered into the concrete box and leave with little Anna for the house on Walnut Hill Avenue.

The air in the house when we return is unnaturally clear without my uncle's cigar smoke. Alice has no one to argue politics with and begins to waste away. She stops crocheting and knitting and her hands begin to stiffen. She also feels guilty for all the traps she's laid in the past for my guileless uncle and regrets the practical jokes she has given him for his birthdays and Christmas. So what if he teased her shamelessly when she was young; he, after all, was young then, too.

My aunt and Mrs. Loop also feel guilty; he was, after all, their husband and cousin, respectively. He was their own kin. How abominably they had treated him at times! Was it his fault he was so boorish? Didn't his mother have something to do with it? Didn't she spoil him shamelessly? Didn't his three cousins, Mrs. Loop, her sister, May, and Alice, have something to do with it? No one becomes a despicable boor all by himself.

Guilt, that most universal of all human gifts, pervades the house, touches even little Anna since she remembers all too well the dozens and dozens of murders she committed upon her uncle and burns with shame over them still.

Aunt Lila, having no husband now, turns her icy tongue on Anna and Mrs. Loop and even at times on Alice.

There is something missing from the house. A scapegoat is missing, a post for whipping, an object on which to sharpen one's claws. Perhaps there will arise from these four women, Aunt Lila, Mrs. Loop, Alice, and little Anna, a new scapegoat, a new whipping post. Perhaps it will be Alice.

Perhaps it will be little Anna.

The bugle sounds "Reveille" again. And again. We three hurry to the door, my scalp tingling as though recently sandblasted. Mrs. Loop calls back over her shoulder to Alice that we are all about to depart for our trip downtown to eat our lunch at Stouffer's. Alice bawls loudly from her spot on the back porch not to forget to bring her back a piece of Stouffer's chocolate pie, that she certainly does like Stouffer's chocolate pie.

Alas, Mrs. Loop, as excellent a cook as she is, could not bake Alice's birthday cake herself in her big gas oven, the problem being Alice's housebound state. How could Mrs. Loop set about such a task, as pleasant as it might be, with Alice tooling aimlessly around the house in her wheelchair, looking for crannies and hiding places on the back or the front porch or out by the new picket fence so that she might not look on at the creation of her own surprise? The cake must come into the house, instead, mysteriously and beautifully wrapped in colored tissue paper and opened in front of us all at the appropriate time and the candles, at this time exactly forty, carefully placed in their holders around the side, and lit and sung over and blown out by Alice.

My, but the cake was huge! I had never seen, nor have I seen since a cake so large for any member of any of the families with whom I have had the dubious pleasure of living for months or weeks, or sometimes years at a time. No, I've never seen a cake so huge—iced with a thick, creamy white icing, bouquets of sugary coral roses ringing the edge, each one nestled in three apple-green leaves, the cake two feet in diameter, and inscribed in Old English lettering, the words:

Alice—we love you.

* * *

Alice, I love you, I really do. I can't look directly at you; your bawling voice makes my stomach shrink with pain. I touch your pale and misshapen fingers with fearful reluctance as you slip the thread back into position and lay the crochet hook properly into my hand.

But Alice, I love you.

I really do.

IV

I am sitting here in the furthest left-hand corner of the back seat of my uncle's Packard as it hums through the traffic streaming out of downtown Philadelphia. We are on the way home from our Saturday shopping trip. The trunk is full of packages for Alice, all segregated carefully from her precious and magnificent cake. Mrs. Loop sits beside me in the back, staring resolutely out the window on the right-hand side of the car. In other words, she is looking resolutely away from her younger cousin, my uncle, who is sitting behind the wheel up front, expertly guiding his cream and black instrument in and out of the traffic while he puffs furiously and impotently on his cigar.

I, myself, am holding stomach, heart, and lungs in readiness for a new outburst which I pray fervently will never come to pass.

Actually, the trip downtown was uneventful, if one disregards completely the terrifying verbal sword fight between Mrs. Loop and my uncle, each of them stabbing back and forth, kitty-cornered in the car from Mrs. Loop's place in the back to my uncle's place in the front, he swiveling his head back toward her at regular intervals, spitting out rebuttals and counter-rebuttals through the cigar clenched between his teeth, each accompanied by abrupt whiffs of aromatic tobacco smoke.

Sitting straight and correct, her dark felt hat tilted stylishly over her forehead, my Aunt Lila interjects a warning: if the two of them didn't shut up and my uncle attend to his driving we will all spend Alice's birthday in traction at Philadelphia General Hospital.

The argument stemmed from the following: it seems that my uncle made a decision all on his own, several weeks before, thinking that he was perfectly capable of doing so. Mrs. Loop was on a trip to visit her sister May in Baltimore, unaware that a question might come up at the lumber yard in her absence. As a consequence, Loop's Lumber Yard now has three carloads of rough grade plywood overwhelming its already bulging storage areas where it should have had to accomodate only three *cartons*.

The telephone call from the frantic yard boss came just as we were leaving the house; Mrs. Loop went back to answer it while my uncle continued to blow the car's bugle in exasperation.

There's plywood everywhere, the yard boss had told her. It's blocking access to the number one common pipe, the cedar siding, the two-by-fours, the four-by-fours, the hardwood flooring in the barns, and it's spilled out on the sidewalk and on to the gravel shoulder of Sixth Street.

It'll never be sold, Mrs. Loop tells her cousin later in the car; not in ten years will it be sold, not in twenty years. Her small voice is frighteningly penetrating in the confines of the smoke-filled car.

The yard boss always exaggerates; he outright lies, my uncle shoots back at her. There couldn't possibly be that much goddam plywood in three carloads. No, not even in four carloads.

My aunt's comments become more and more icy. Would my

uncle like to give up his place of honor behind this black and cream bitch of a car upon which he continually wastes his time like a child obsessed with a tinkertoy and let her drive so that he can think his rejoinders out a bit more logically?

His grunt of derision fills the car with several cubic feet of stinging cigar smoke.

Continuing to look straight ahead, my aunt grunts back at him, managing to multiply the scorn contained therein at least one-hundred-fold over his own while at the same time hanging the smoke-filled air with icicles.

Of course he would not allow anyone to touch his precious toy! she says. And how many necessities had they done without in order for him to buy the thing and adorn it, permanently stalled as he is at pre-puberty?

My uncle growls into the windshield, oblivious to these gross insults which he had obviously heard hundreds of times before and expects to hear for the rest of his life. The two of them, he says, should be grateful that he was taking them downtown in the first place. It was his car; he bought it with his own money. Didn't he work for a living from eight to five every day of the week except Saturdays and Sundays, or has he been mistaken all these years? And didn't he have a right to his own hobby? This car happened to be his hobby. Didn't they have their hobbies, stupid as they may be? Did either one of them ever hear him ridicule their stupid-ass hobbies?

And what if he happened to make a small mistake? (A sharp exclamation from the back of the car.) It's nothing, he says, that can't be righted—say, with a big campaign, a carload sale of some kind, advertising all over South Philadelphia, downtown, out to Bryn Mawr, maybe even Upper Darby.

Gratitude is something foreign to both of them, he grumbles. Gratitude to the man—a crack salesman—keeping the family business going. All right, he pronounces into the windshield through puffs of smoke, his voice betraying grievous hurt, if his dear cousin so prefers, he'll resign immediately and he and Lila can go elsewhere. (Aunt Lila turns her head away from him.) There were other lumber yards crying for him. Why, just yesterday the owner of the T&P Lumber Yard in Norristown begged him to consider taking over the branch in Conshohocken . . .

Conshohocken! my aunt exclaims coldly.

. . . the branch, you hear? Not just the goddam measly floor, the whole goddam branch!

Mrs. Loop, he continues, will never be anything but her own stubborn self, just like her husband whose business sense she should know by now he had always deplored as asinine and self-defeating . . .

Mrs. Loop rolls her eyes to the ceiling. The ass! she exclaims. The complete and utter ass!

. . . so fearful is she, he goes on, of anyone showing himself more able than herself to run the business, she steadfastly refuses to relinquish the reins to him, her cousin, who could enlarge the business to three times its present size.

To Mrs. Loop, it was obvious: it was impossible for my uncle to make a decision without blasting everything to hell and gone. For instance, that load of nutless bolts he ordered last year; and the customer from West Chester whose order he lost not once, but three times—an order amounting to the sum total of $3,500.

Smoke is everywhere in the car, drifting out the windows in clouds, fogging the windshield.

My aunt implores them to leave off; she's rapidly developing a headache. But no, Mrs. Loop remembers the time my uncle nearly burned down the garage playing with matches when he was already ten years old and should have known better . . .

That's it, my uncle blasts back at her, bring up the past; dig everything out of that tomb of a brain of yours . . .

. . . and his mother called the fire department and blamed arsonists for the deed, because that was the third fire in the neighborhood that week . . .

Aunt Lila continued to argue for an end to the thing. Aren't they preparing for Alice's birthday? What condition will they be in to make any kind of decisions, good or ill, regarding what to get for her? Could they all for once go somewhere together without having an argument?

* * *

All this time I sit as still as a ball of dust in the back of the car hoping that they had all forgotten about me, as indeed they probably had. But you know how it is with children. They're there and if things go badly, that is, if it's evident that an adult is losing an argument utterly and there is nowhere else to strike out, and there happens to be a child handy, in the absence of a dog or an unsuspecting cat, or at least a solid wall to kick without damage, the child will surely get it. Haven't I lived through an entire childhood, haven't I lived through grownup arguments by the dozens, haven't we all?

And so I sat and trembled while I listened to them, unable to escape when I was eleven and when I was twelve, thirteen, fourteen, fifteen, and I flinched when they noticed me . . .

Straighten up there must you slouch in your seat all the time let me see your fingernails didn't I tell you this morning to make sure your fingernails were clean I'm ashamed to be seen with you ungrateful disgusting don't you know we see you looking at all the boys those pimply-faced boys I don't know why I'm saddled with a girl like you ungrateful troublemaker leaving your bed unmade eating all the time growing out of your clothes disobedient impudent sure to bring home a bastard baby sending me to the grave . . .

* * *

In approximately five minutes I am to recite the seventh to tenth articles of faith to Mrs. Loop, my catechist, who has completely recovered, so far as I can see, from her noontime free-for-all with my uncle. She is now as warm and benevolent as a Sister of Charity, sitting here beside me on the back porch. Some mysterious solution must have been arrived at between my uncle and her and the yard boss. Would she be wound down sufficiently to hear me recite? Can I remember even a word of my catechism after all that fire and smoke and brimstone in the car this afternoon? I have been rereading the four articles frantically as I sit here and they appear to me as foreign as something out of the *Koran*.

Now then, Mrs. Loop says to me, where were we to begin? She takes the small pamphlet from my hand and I look sideways at the eyes behind her rimless glasses. I never noticed before that, though her eyes appear very small behind her glasses, they are really quite large. I have the sudden compulsion to ask her to remove her glasses so that I could see, so to speak, inside her.

Alice is not very difficult to see, though her pale blue, swimming eyes are painful to look at. Everything touches her, everything opens her self to inspection. Love me, she says, I am good, I am kind. I am intelligent. I wish to do everything I can to make you happy. I will lay my life down for the sake of your small feet that they may have something gentle to walk on.

But Mrs. Loop. Is she full of blood-red rage, held down as it were with an iron claw? I expected her in the car to break free from herself at any moment and pound my uncle's dapper head to a bloody pulp with the umbrella she was holding. Could such rage as I saw this afternoon escape some day? Might it be directed at little Anna for some infraction, some lapse in memory, some downright immoral act on her part? Ah, fear—the universal parasite of humanity, eating away at the brain's soft tissue, at the stomach's lining, at the twenty-to-twenty-five feet of intestines; fear, the child's intimate, her alter ego, her *doppelgänger*.

* * *

Miraculously, I remember all four articles for Mrs. Loop, with only a modicum of stumbling, mostly over pronunciation. Last week we talked about confession, a ritual occasionally observed by members of the High Episcopal Church, and in my muddled interpretation of this mysterious observance I wondered often during the weeks following my uncle's bedroom visit if perhaps I could confess to the vicar—that faceless man whom I had seen no closer than twenty-five feet distant—and not only get some sin off my conscience but at the same time get my uncle's unsettling and unending scrutiny off my back through some miracle of priestly intercession.

Alas, it is not to be. Mrs. Loop pats my knee affectionately and tells me that little girls like Anna are not expected to confess so early in their instruction. Besides, she goes on, Anna would not have any sin to speak of, at any rate. And on that I would agree with her—not to *speak of*.

I look at my nunlike catechist, Mrs. Loop, still dressed in her business-brown, for what is a very long time for me, shifty-eyed as I have become in the last four weeks. She is fingering through my catechism. Now she looks up to see my eyes upon her and smiles her small, bright smile at me and assigns me the next three articles. She does not suggest that if I had need of confession, that I might confess to her.

V

I am thirteen now and back in Hudders Wharf. The grass and trees are very still. There are no cars going up and down the street bordering the Delaware River, for the morning shipyard traffic is already past and it's still too early for shoppers to be going to downtown Camden, fifteen miles away. A solitary bus rumbles by, going the other way, toward Williamstown. One rider is sitting in the very back.

The August sun is warm on my legs.

Aunt Lila and my uncle are far away, relatively speaking, across the river in Philadelphia, and I have lived here in my new home for two years.

Mrs. Loop is most likely still at the lumber yard in South Philadelphia, watching that orders go out correctly, that accounts are paid on time, that shipments do not appear one-hundred-fold in excess.

Aunt Lila said that she did not want to see me again, and left the packing of all the new clothes she had made for me in the hands of Mrs. Loop and Alice. Mrs. Loop was sure that my aunt would someday relent, but even she, and Alice too, even Alice, were nonplussed by my outburst that day: I hate you, I hate you, I had cried at them all. How could I hate them, they wondered? They had given me all of their love.

My Aunt Lila, for all her aloofness, Mrs. Loop explained, had wished very much to make me her daughter. And fearfully expecting me to scorn her as my mother, was heartbroken all the more when it appeared that I did just that.

It was unfortunate that I left right before the projected trip to Atlantic City. It was not that I wished so much for the trip itself, for we were to go as was inevitable in my uncle's smoky, quarrelsome car, but that the four of us were to be together there—I mean, Mrs. Loop, Aunt Lila, Alice, and I. They were going to take Alice in the front seat, in Aunt Lila's place, her wheelchair folded up in the trunk. Alice, sitting beside me on the back porch, talked of the wonders that we would see—of Hammond's Pier, for instance, and of towering, sprawling, white hotels, circled around with pink and blue hydrangeas, and miles and miles of boardwalk. Of course we would get salt water taffy to bring back with us, and would eat popcorn and cotton candy while walking the stretch from Hammond's to Steele Pier.

We were to go to Atlantic City the next weekend, I to run into the combers while Mrs. Loop, Aunt Lila, and my uncle rested under an umbrella and Alice sat in the shade of the pavilion by the boardwalk.

We were to go to Atlantic City.

* * *

The Old Man my mother had forbidden me to talk to during the weeks before she entered the hospital I may now go to visit with impunity. I am a grownup girl of thirteen, a junior candy-striper, visiting the elderly with a bag of peanut butter cookies bought at Loebson's delicatessen down at the corner with part of my baby-sitting money.

My new foster mother, Mrs. Donaghy, gives not a thought to the old senile nuisance, it's the pimply-faced boys she worries about, the hair-brained cheerleaders, too, who might lure me into their degenerate midst, the smart-ass misses who try out for the class play and debate team. She knows! She knows very well what goes on during those trips to Patterson and Glassboro and Passaic.

That of course shoots all extra-curricular activities at school, even if I had the nerve, the looks, the intelligence, the talent, to try out for them. But I can talk to the Old Man, the poor old bastard, as Mrs. Donaghy refers to him. Who in hell, she says, would want to bother with the old geezer anyway?

But I'm fortunate in my new foster mother—lacking as she might be in the gentler emotions, suspicious as she might be of all people under the age of fifty-five, pinched and grumbling and able to call up a storehouse of grievances against anyone and everyone, especially teenage girls but also government agencies, the public schools, the Protestants, Catholics, and Jews—for she is nevertheless a widow and brotherless and fatherless. Later on, I will look back with nostalgia to this particular period of my life.

* * *

The old hotel rises in front of me, dark green, looking out across the river with blind, shade-drawn eyes, except for the captain's three windows. He's sitting on the upper porch, leaning over his mandolin, tightening the strings, trying the sound, looking back and forth from the pick in his hand to the fingerboard. I walk to the outside steps on River Street and climb up to him. The captain looks around and raises his bristly eyebrows and smiles through his yellowing mustache and beard and says, why, hello.

He straightens a little and pulls a rocker closer to him, so much like Alice did at the beginning of each crocheting lesson with her, and like Mrs. Loop did before my catechism recital, that my chest and throat feel tight and full.

The molasses-colored shell of his mandolin glistens in the morning sun. He moves his wrinkled fist over the strings slowly, plucking at random with his celluloid pick, and pushing out his lips silently while he watches the fingerboard. A tug whistle blows and we both look up. A big cargo ship has come abreast of us, kept in line by three little tugs, their rope bumpers matty-looking and wet. There's another tug on the other side, trailing behind. It's this tug that has been sounding its whistle.

Portuguese, the old man pronounces, nodding toward the ship. And then he adds with authority, loaded with cork. A flat statement, full of unconscious dignity, drifting out to touch the Portuguese ship like a blessing.

We both watch the ship and the tugs. The one trailing behind is sounding its whistle almost frantically, as though not wishing to be left. I suddenly remember my cookies and rattle the bag open and offer them wordlessly to the old man. He raises his eyebrows again, reaches into the bag, murmurs a thank you, and extracts three of them. He slips his pick between the strings on the neck of his mandolin and we sit silently, the two of us, Springtime and December, Heidi and Grandfather, Youth and Experience, eating our cookies and looking out over the water at the ship and tugs moving slowly toward north Philadelphia. A sailboat scuds downriver, there and gone in half the time it took the others.

The old man breathes in sharply: Aaaaahhh. And after a little while he says, my sloop could outrun them all. I've told you about my sloop, haven't I? He turns to me vaguely.

At Hammond's Pier, he goes on, looking again out over the water, they put a wreath around my neck; red and white roses it was. And the crowds that were there that day! I told you about them, didn't I? I never saw so many people, all of them yelling and laughing and clapping and some of them crying, my crew and my friends, laughing and crying.

And I was crying, too; crying after Cape May, after the hurricane that hit Cape May, my sloop like matchsticks all over the rocks, crying . . .

He's quiet for a while and then he says, that was the last race, that one at Hammond's Pier—have I ever told you that?—the last race before Cape May. And then he stops abruptly, and when I turn to him, he's looking down, somewhat shrunken into himself. Then he begins to pluck at his mandolin and sing. His unsteady voice wavers thinly on the river breeze:

> Oh matey, my matey,
> Oh where have you gone?

And the sound carries me away, away from this good man, away to an unknown watery world, and I am eleven, thirteen, thirty-two.

> Oh matey, my matey,
> Oh where have you gone?

The old man's cheeks are wet beneath his tufted eyebrows as he leans there, over his mandolin, this good man sorrowing, his fist unmoving on the strings. For him, perhaps, I am not there. I cry, too, as though alone myself, the two of us mingling our tears over things irretrievably lost, utterly out of the grasp of our begging hands. Atlantic City, he says, and his voice still wavers. And then he says it again, Atlantic City—like a lost life, a lost feasibility, a lost possibility of germination and flowering and maturing with those three women, all so different, all so loving and hating in their own ways, those three women in Philadelphia so long ago.

* * *

Isn't she sweet, such a sweet little thing, so young, so pure. Isn't she innocent? Isn't she helpless? A ruddy, dark-eyed baby, her smoky hair brushed up into a curl at the top of her head, her small grasping hands clenched into fists, sucking at my breast frantically, hungrily. I would kill for her; I would kill anyone who dared approach as though to harm her. I would kill with a joy that could not possibly be contained, strangle and tear apart . . . I would kill, yes, have killed, over and over, ground my teeth and clenched my fists, strangled and kicked, frantic for her safety, for her beauty, her innocence, her complete and utter lack of rage and hate, her laugh, her joy, her round little belly, her small, budding breasts, following the geese across the yard, quietly, so as not to startle them, intent on the gosling falling back from the rest. My chest swells with protectiveness; I grow hot with rage. Who would dare to harm her, who would dare?

And what harm did it do to her precious lumber yard, my uncle growls into the windshield, what if I made a small mistake? It's nothing that couldn't be righted—say, with a big campaign, a whopper of a sale all over Philadelphia . . . it's all over Philadelphia how she had let him into her bedroom while her aunt was innocently away on a visit to Baltimore. The little slut, they grow up quickly these days. Actually, you can't trust these girls, none of them.

Ah, little Anna, how they have wronged you! Come to me, Anna. Let me close you up in my arms.

* * *

The shadows of the limbs and leaves grope across the ninon curtains in my tower bedroom. It's very early in the morning but already warm and pleasant in Philadelphia. Four weeks ago I was introduced to my first male instrument—my uncle's. It's nice, you know, to keep that sort of experience in the family. How odd it looked—dark red and stiff and veering off to the right and I wondered in my eleven-year-old numb skull if the female vagina must not veer off similarly in order to accomodate such a phenomenon. Fortunately, this particular riddle I never, in his or my particular case that night, fully solved—for my uncle's intention at this time was a less painful exploration, he of me and I of him, leaving my virginity as it were intact for the time being. He began as many of the how-to books tell us we should, with a night of foreplay. And he took this opportunity as we might expect him to, cosmopolitan as he is, to practice his French, both high school and unconventional.

Ah, cherie, ma petite . . . no one could understand how he felt, they would pervert this pure love of his into something vulgar. I must therefore never discuss it, must act as usual—until the next time. This is our first time together, *ma cherie*, the first of many. And the things we will do! The things you will see! One of which—and like a magician he lifts the open flap of his red and white striped pajamas—is *this!*

Touch it, Anna. Isn't it hard, though, isn't it big! Guess who did that to me Anna, he says with pop eyes hugely innocent, guess what naughty little girl did that?

* * *

The bucket my mother carries is crawling with crabs fresh from the ocean. It's the summer before my father's death in October 1940 and my mother has just pulled in the traps and is walking back across the sand, weaving in and out between the clumps of dune grass with the bucket in her hand. She takes the bucket to the sink in the kitchen and turns the water on, letting it fill and the water run over the side and down the drain, the crabs turning over and over in the continually moving stream.

Mother's dark hair is pulled back into a soft bun like Aunt Lila's except that my mother's hair has a deep curl. Little tendrils are brushing her cheeks and escaping under the bun at the nape of her neck; her forehead and neck are covered with fine beads of sweat from the work of the pier and the walk back in the afternoon heat. Her arms are very dark from the sun.

I'm disappointed that she hadn't told me she was going, having spent the afternoon alone, building towns with twigs and shells and stones in the sandy front yard, sullen and marooned, not knowing where she had gone and afraid to go off searching for her for fear she'd come back another way and not find me and fly into a fit of worry and chasing here and there, calling my name wildly, sure I had drowned or been kidnapped or killed by some passing madman, and having found me finally behind some sand dune not twenty feet from the house, struggling up out of a huge hole I had dug, or by the tiny inlet, paddling with bare feet in the water heated by the sun, catch me up in her arms and weep with frustration at me and relief that I was still alive—causing her, as usual, no end of anxiety of which she had too much already, what with my sick father and all.

And it was my Aunt Lila, my cool, almost unflappable Aunt Lila who ran away at age sixteen to play Little Eva in *Uncle Tom's Cabin*! While my mercurial mother, jumping from laughter to anger to frenzy to melancholy at the average rate of one jump per waking hour, stayed home like a sensible girl and married my thirty-year-old storekeeper father at twenty-one and waited ten years, until after the two of them could afford to build this oceanside house, to have a child.

I now put the kettle of water on the stove while my mother quickly pares potatoes and slices them up into a pot. I am set to spreading the kitchen table with oilcloth. Then Mother lifts the bucket and coaxes the crabs into the sink, slips the stopper into the drain with the long tongs, and pours the now heated water from the tea kettle over them. The crabs stop moving and lie lazily on the bottom of this hot sea, awaiting their fate dumbly.

Mother scrubs them with the vegetable brush and puts them on the rack in the blue agateware pot. She adds a little water and a half glass of beer and sprinkles them all over with red pepper.

She works rapidly, her hands are slim and sure, her nails cut short and filed to perfect points. The blue wrap-around dress covers her loosely, the belt tied in a knot in the front. On her feet are a pair of worn sneakers that were at one time white but are now stained and gray with beach tar.

She will make Dutch potato salad out of the cooked potatoes and we two will eat that and the crabs, cracking the claws and prying the shells up to get at the white, sweet meat inside. My mother will drink the rest of the beer and I will drink orangeade. We will soon be almost too stuffed to move.

Afterwards we will walk along the beach, the sun slanting across the tops of the dune grass, baking us on one side while the breeze from the ocean lifts our hair and blows our dresses against our legs on the other.

My mother will constantly rub her hands together as though brushing away sand, will bend to pick up a shell and throw it out toward the water, rub her hands together again and again, and squint into the distance. She will be thinking of my father.

The store in Cape May has been sold to pay bills; we are living on the rest. Soon my mother will have to move us closer to Camden and find a job.

* * *

They are eating crab and potato salad, the table is spread with oilcloth, they crack the claws and lift up the apron to get at the white flesh underneath.

The oilcloth is on the table, and the child is choking on a piece of shell; the father puts his finger inside her mouth to find it. The child, Anna, is in the highchair. The scene is cobwebby and distant. I see it over and over again, I taste his finger in my mouth, I feel his other hand tight on my shoulder, I hear him and my mother speaking together fearfully, I sense the urgency and concern in his voice. I am sure he will help me, I feel comforted, my father—he was a good man. The nurse is holding my wrist, a voice says in the whiteness: her respiration is very low, her heart . . . a fifty-year-old heart is not so strong that it can withstand such a dose of Seconal . . .

The scenes are cobwebby and distant and vaguely white, but nevertheless are real. It happened—did it not?—it all happened.

I see my father, a muscular man in a long apron, his sandy head is thrown back in laughter, his two strong hands rest on the counter. There are customers in the store—an old man and a woman—and my mother is at the candy case, unpacking boxes. They are all laughing in the store with my father.

He holds me in his arms in front of the Christmas tree and touches the silvery angel on top. Anna, he says. We will call the angel "Anna".

I am my father's angel. Can he see my need to talk to him? Run away Anna, he says, run away from this uncle of yours. Put this Satan behind you.

VI

At the head of the table, my uncle eats the same way as he drives his cream and black Packard through the downtown traffic—with consummate efficiency and unconcern. Naturally he is finished eating before anyone else. He takes up his cigar while waiting for dessert, puffs out huge clouds of smoke as he lights it, and then leans back and a little sideways in his chair to obtain a clear view of his car parked outside under the oak tree.

He is smiling very slightly, but defensively, or perhaps guardedly. He gives that impression—that he is always on guard, like the outside hound who finds his way accidentally through a half-opened screen door into the kitchen, and though appearing to be brazenly taking his ease on the round carpet in front of the kitchen table directly in the path of the sun coming through the window, is nevertheless waiting every minute for the broom or the rolled-up newspaper to signal his ignominious return to the kennel behind the garages next to the garbage cans.

My uncle, for all his bravado, for all his French whisperings in the dark that night, treads lightly in this house. His feet fall quietly on the stairs that lead down to his apartment in his loose, needlepoint carpet slippers, given to him for his birthday by Alice.

Run away, Anna, my father whispers to me from beyond the grave. The words swirl deliciously around me, I read them over and over in a novel I write in my head, full of adventure, of risk to myself; I lie in bed at night, living and re-living my escape, I know exactly how I will do it. I slip stealthily down the stairs, my sandals are in my hand, the house is huge with darkness, my suitcase is packed, actually packed; I play this game to the hilt. I have come to the end of my tether, I don't know what else to do.

I slip out the back door on Monday and put my suitcase under the back porch just behind the steps, right next to my aunt's bed of lavender. The case has in it my new silk panties, my pink and white dress, three nightgowns, and a book of short stories by Ellery Queen which I extracted from Alice's shelves the night before.

The next move is utterly beyond me. Do I want to leave this haven? Might not my uncle die next Sunday? Could I not simply bolt my bedroom door? Could my uncle and I work out some less incestuous arrangement? But the problem is solved for me, and all at once—my aunt discovers the suitcase on Tuesday.

* * *

One of the disappointments of my Aunt Lila's life, my mother told me once, was her failure to have a child. And Lila's relationship with my mother changed when I was born—there rose up between them a coolness beginning with my successful birth, that my mother seemed never able to dispel. Whenever they were together after that, it was as though I came between them—my existence, that is—so that my early memories of Aunt Lila are of a handsome woman, reserved and unapproachable, a woman of whom I was a little frightened.

But my mother insisted to me that Lila loved me dearly and wanted as dearly for me to love her. And indeed I would often see her, when I glanced up from something I was doing, looking at me intently, her eyes almost fathomless in their darkness. But she never cultivated me. It was as though I must prove to her in some subtle way that I wanted her to love me and that I loved her, in turn, very much.

Was I ever able to do this? Did I understand fully the pain and need hidden deep in my lovely Aunt Lila, the fear and even assurance she had of rejection? She would never reach out and ask for it; I must bring my love to her in my hands.

* * *

The table stands longways in front of the big bay window which looks out on the side yard, now largely in the shade of the house since it is six o'clock in the evening, and Saturday is nearly gone. There are almost two days to go before I will pack my suitcase, after which events will take care of themselves.

At the head of the table sits my uncle, puffing on his cigar and looking out the window at his Packard. His blue eyes are smoldering as though his head ached; he's brooding on life and its many frustrations. He will go out to his car and ride down the Mediterranean coast to the Riviera, to Cannes. He can already feel the sea air whipping his hair about. Will his brakes fail on the next curve, I wonder, plunging him over the cliff?

Mrs. Loop is finishing up the last of her *béarnaise* sauce which she has stirred into her rice. Alice is sipping her coffee. I have yet to finish the pile of broccoli on my plate, not my favorite food, even with the extra butter slipped to me by Alice who is sitting beside me at the table.

My Aunt Lila is sitting with her hands lying loosely in her lap, looking out the little squares of the window at something far away. Perhaps she is forseeing our confrontation in my bedroom the following Tuesday, knowing of course that something of the kind would happen between us, for some reason or other—eventually.

She is facing me as I sit rigidly on the window seat of my bedroom and I am looking sullenly, it seems, down at my hands, my red hands, caught red handed, but of course it could be worse. The thing with my uncle, for instance, so irrevocably bound up with the suitcase, if I should slip and tell her about the thing with my uncle . . .

Aunt Lila holds the suitcase beside her, looking at me, and for my Aunt Lila makes an astonishing concession—she opens herself up to hurt, unbuttons her breast, as it were, like a sweater, and shows her heart to me—a pearl before swinishness, beauty and love before a hound of a puppy unable to grasp the first word of what she was asking—Don't you like living here? she asks. Do you want to go back to Hudders Wharf? (*Don't you love me at all? she asks. Shall I never be anyone's mother?*) She is holding herself tense for the answer, she is braced for the sting of my hand.

I look sullenly into my lap, tears spilling over my eyelashes, dumb with the knowledge that I am dumb, that I have no words, no spontaneity that would send me hurtling toward her with my arms outstretched for the comfort I know I would have received, that would have been torn out of Aunt Lila with the suddenness of a thunderclap, and with that cataclysm, healing us both at once. I look into my lap, tears spilling over my eyelashes and onto my hands, and know that my silence has broken Aunt Lila's heart.

I am led at length down to the kitchen for an audience with the rest of the family. It's Tuesday evening; Mrs. Loop looks at me, worry and puzzlement all over her face, fresh from her office and now standing before the stove about to cook supper. Alice sits in her wheelchair, loose mouth slightly open. My uncle puffs furiously on his cigar in the back doorway.

She does not *have* to leave, pronounces my aunt coldly, as though I were not in the room.

Does she *want* to leave? asks Mrs. Loop.

Do you *want* to leave? growls my uncle, filling the space before him with cigar smoke, obscuring for a moment his blue pop-eyes, his slippery, persistent tongue.

I turn to my uncle, the cause of it all. My chest swells with wretchedness—to have it all ruined so soon, to have him still living and breathing! Grief sears my eyes, my face; rage boils up in my throat—Yes! I answer him, trembling all over, my voice very small in the silent room. I hold myself rigid before them like an animal at bay and look at my uncle's widening eyes. I hate you, I whisper, knowing this life is over. And in the futile defiance that comes from the sure knowledge that there is nothing left to lose, I raise my voice higher—I hate you, I say. And higher—*I hate you, I hate you!*

I turn in a half-circle, my words raking over them all, over these women who could never understand what it was that I needed to tell them—*I hate you, I hate you!* I turn away from them and run out of the room, I pound up the back stairs like someone demented and careen through Alice's room, crying it over and over—*I hate you, I hate you!* I run up the narrow steps through the tower, through the door of my room, and throw myself on my bed. I repeat it again and again to myself as I lie there—I hate you, I say, I hate you. I repeat it until I run down from exhaustion—I hate you, I hate you.

I hate you.

* * *

The debate goes on for two days—what should they do about Anna? My uncle is deeply and thoroughly hurt, my aunt is no longer speaking to anyone, Alice will not stop weeping. Mrs. Loop is left to handle the problem—a frustrating one indeed, for Anna refuses to eat and answers every question with the same implacable statement: *I want to go back to Hudders Wharf.*

Mrs. Loop contacts the welfare office there at last and arranges for my move across the river. A certain amount is deposited in trust with a Hudders Wharf lawyer to help with my education. She tries to explain the circumstances to these people in Hudders Wharf but she can't understand the problem, she can't see what they've done wrong, they have treated me as one of their own, they have given me all of their love.

I have broken all of their hearts.

* * *

The table is heavy oak with a single pedestal in the middle, from which radiate four heavy claw-footed legs. It is round and sits directly under a stained glass chandelier which hangs from the middle of the room. Mrs. Barker sits across from me, her intricately lined face reflecting only her interest in the pork and applesauce which remain on her plate. We are to have custard for dessert. I get up from the table to bring a dish of it back for each of us.

Oh, thank you my dear, says Mrs. Barker to me. I get home much later now since starting office practice as a clerk at Armstrong Cork Company, a branch office with a dock on the Delaware River and a large storage yard. I get ten dollars every week for the work I do which is part of my school curriculum and is meant to prepare me for a paying job. I have been buying some of my own clothes and have acquired a very tentative feeling of being adult. Mrs. Barker has helped in this respect.

I have just turned seventeen.

A choir leader in a church I attended persuaded Mrs. Barker, a widow, to take me in as a foster child/boarder for the last year of my under-aged life, and put an end to my rootless existence in Hudders Wharf since Mrs. Donaghy's heart attack three years before. Mrs. Barker looks upon me as a paying boarder, nothing less, accepting my help with preparing meals, dishwashing, laundry, and cleaning with mild surprise and pleasure.

The house is a bungalow crowded among many others on a tree-shaded street on the outskirts of Hudders Wharf. Mrs. Barker has a candy and notions store in the front of her house where she spends a good part of the day and evening.

I have a small, pleasant room, furnished with a bookcase for my books and even a desk. I have been here for several months. After I graduate from high school next week, I may continue at Armstrong Cork, perhaps in a more responsible position, at twenty-five dollars a week. Perhaps I will stay on with Mrs. Barker as a full-fledged boarder.

The neighborhood is quiet and respectable. Mrs. Barker and I go to St. Stephen's Episcopal Church together on Sunday by bus and come home together afterward, talking about the music that was played and sung. Mrs. Barker comments on the sermon, most especially on its length. She laughs easily.

Mrs. Barker has a bachelor brother, Percy, the seventh and youngest in a family which accumulated six girls before him. Three of the sisters are still alive, Mrs. Barker included. The other two sisters have disowned their brother, so Mrs. Barker feels obliged to take him in when he needs a home; that is, when he loses his job, or after he has spent a certain number of days or weeks or months in the hospital or jail. This happens, she tells me, quite often. He has a room in the basement.

Her brother's trouble, she says, stems from a speech impediment he has that is somehow connected to an extreme underbite. This is a misfortune, she says, especially for a man. He also has a glandular problem which makes him overweight.

This story, related quietly in the third month of my life with Mrs. Barker, depresses me, and I look forward to this brother's next appearance in her house with a kind of resignation. Each of my previous and temporary foster homes came equipped with a problem male, precipitating me into the welfare office to beg for relocation: three moves in three years. I had hoped Mrs. Barker's would be my last stop.

* * *

It's a month later. Mrs. Barker's brother is no match for me, but rather a mild irritation, bothering me at times with a little uneasiness, that's all, a little disgust, a great disgust really, a monumental contempt at times.

His eyes are blood-shot. The air is heavy with the odor of whiskey and garlic as he leans over me. The kitchen table rocks and my teacup spills tea all over the porcelain top. His sister calls him sharply from the next room, but he has by now a firm hold on my hand and his grin is full of promise—of lovely things, exciting things, things only *he* can give me.

His sister comes to the door. Percy, she says, Percy . . . How can she stand this man, her brother, I think, and looking back and forth from one to the other of them I become filled with loathing.

I move shortly after this to a rooming house within walking distance of Armstrong Cork and make up my mind to live alone for the rest of my life.

And at times throughout the years, sitting on the bus, watching the men around me covertly from under my eyelashes, looking at the boys in my high school and college classes, at my friend's father, at a neighbor (even looking at those who become most precious to me, at my husband, for instance, or at my son-in-law), I wonder if they are all like Mr. Barker's brother or like my uncle. I can barely suppress the disgust that wells up inside me at these times; I was indeed helpless once, I think to myself, but now I will make them pay and pay.

It never enters my mind that the ones who will pay are not necessarily those who had incurred the original debt. That was incurred years before when I could hardly bring myself to look at them all each morning—my aunt and Alice and Mrs. Loop. Couldn't they see it written all over my face—the guilt and rage that lay there ever since that night with my uncle?

The guilt alone would keep me from confessing the thing then, even to Alice. How can I? How can I confess it rightly without going right down to the last detail, because of course, they would ask about everything, they would insist that I describe it all, wondering to themselves whether in the final analysis I had precipitated the whole thing myself.

The bright light goes on, the grilling begins, my feet dangle from the dark, high-backed witness box chair. The prosecutor is merciless. The jury is too embarrassed to look at me. The verdict comes in: guilty, twelve to zero. The judge is ready to pronounce sentence.

* * *

Mrs. Loop and I are traveling across the Delaware River bridge on the number forty-two bus. We must be at the welfare office in Hudders Wharf at two o'clock in order to meet Mrs. Donaghy, a veteran in the field of bringing up recalcitrant girls.

Mrs. Loop is staring out the right-hand window on the right-hand side of the bus. My aunt is no doubt sewing at this moment in her workroom, losing herself in her work. My uncle is watching things at the lumber yard in his cousin's absence. Alice was still in bed when we left at noon, reading an Agatha Christie novel, tears cascading from her pale, sea-blue eyes. On Sunday Mrs. Loop will go to mass and pray for my soul and for the soul of Aunt Lila.

The bus is hot and stuffy with cigar smoke and someone is eating peanuts behind us. The struts of the bridge fly by. The toll station will soon appear at the New Jersey side.

* * *

My aunt walks into the dining room, a plate of pie in each hand. The silver hair below her temples contrasts strikingly with her black dress. The dress, which she made herself, hangs from her shoulders and softly gathered waist in delicate folds that move very slightly with each step. I think to myself that I have never seen her look so beautiful.

She puts one plate of pie down in front of my uncle and the other in front of Alice. Her eyes glance over me and she holds up her index finger: mine will come in a minute.

Alice has been talking to me about Hitler, he having been as usual the prime subject of the news broadcast just before we sat down to dinner. She described the man as shallow, crude, and emotionally disturbed.

My uncle interjects a comment amid copious puffs of smoke. The guy is a nut, he says.

Alice attempts to explain to me how such a man could be elected to the head of the German nation—by feeding the German people things they want to hear: that everything will be fine after they get rid of the Communists and Jews; by offering them scapegoats—the conniving Jew, the atheistic Communist.

My uncle thrusts in another smoky comment: they're *all* nuts.

Smoke hangs in clouds and billows over the dining room table.

Aunt Lila, back in the dining room again, sets my pie in front of me and sits down to her own. My uncle takes over the conversation. He removes his cigar, lays it carefully on the tray in front of him, and blows a large plume of smoke out toward the side yard. He admires, he says in a deep summing-up voice, the beliefs of the America First Committee. My aunt rolls her eyes to the ceiling.

My God, interjects Mrs. Loop.

Alice says nothing. Alice is lying in wait until my uncle rolls out his rope to its full length, knots it, lays it loosely around his neck.

What are the beliefs of the America First Committee? asks my aunt. Her voice sounds only slightly interested, as though she asked the question just to keep the conversation going, nothing more. But my uncle is immediately on his guard. He knows very well that my aunt knows all about the America First Committee; she knows all about everything. She sits home all day and does nothing but read the papers, three of them, and listens to the news, and has her own private subscription to the *New Republic*—a magazine that has leftist opinions on everything which it expresses in interminably long sentences. He has often accused her of quoting long sections of it to him verbatim as though they were original with her, just to show him up. Now she's baiting him; she always baits him.

I feel, he says truculently, exactly as the Committee does about keeping out of foreign wars. Let them fight it out themselves, he says. Why should we be bothered with their emotionally disturbed nuts? Europe produced this nut, Hitler; let Europe take care of him.

Alice clears her thick throat: And if this nut should declare war on us? she asks.

My uncle lets explode a laugh, short and derisive. No words necessary here. He has no words to answer such a ridiculous question, no time to consider such a ridiculous possibility.

* * *

And it was a ridiculous possibility, truly ridiculous, that out there in the country, surrounded by church-going neighbors, virtuous and kind, decent and clean, that anyone would possibly touch the girl—or that he would come back, or someone like him, sliding silently across the grass toward her, his hands at the ready to pick her up and carry her off, perhaps to the little grove of trees she liked so much to sit in. And really, it was too much for the girl to grow up with, this constant climate of anxiety. She would feel smothered, she would hate me, she'd run away from home, leaving perhaps a note on the dresser.

What if I told her? What if I explained the thing to her so she would understand my terror, my fear that she might be carried off, touched, fondled, that she will grow up to hate so much, that she might carry with her through all of her life this rage, this nausea and disgust. Perhaps then, if it all came out in the open between us, perhaps then the thing would disappear, and she could have a natural childhood untouched by that darkness I feel, that insane desire to laugh and laugh.

I see my husband in the sheep shed, a muscular man like my father. He rubs the wet newborn lamb with a towel, muttering low sounds to the nuzzling ewe. The lamb fights weakly to stay upright on shaky, silky black legs. My husband smiles through his dark blond beard, thick and short and whitened with frost. The first lamb of the year, he says, and it's a real good size.

He picks the lamb up in his arms and the small black face looks over the denim-covered arm, opens its pink mouth and tongues a plaintive cry into the foggy frost of the stackyard. He carries the lamb through the winter air and the ewe's worried cry follows him. He walks up the back steps, into the warm entry way, to the doorway of the laughing, yellow-lit kitchen. Here! the man calls at the doorway. Here! the first lamb, and so early! The girl, a high school student now, runs out to the kitchen to see him. She is tall and straight as a boy; her oval eyes are dark with black-brown centers.

Her father sets the lamb upright on its four intractable legs. The black muzzle opens and it tongues the air. Maaa! it cries, Maaa! There now, the man says, and leans over and fondles the baby-bone legs, the black silky ears, the wooly sides which are bellying out with sucked-up breath.

The man stands up then, broad and short, looking down at the wooly thing. His beard is tucked into his denim coat, his arms hang at his sides. The girl kneels down. There now, she says (just like her father), there now. She strokes the curly sides of the lamb, she touches the tiny hoof with her slim forefinger. The lamb looks close into the girl's face. Maaa! it cries, Maaa!

My husband, a professor of physics, runs a small farm with his family: a herd of some twenty ewes, lambs in February and March, grass hay in the pasture, a kitchen garden, a small Ford tractor, a one-bottomed plow, a scraper, a mower, an ancient and rusty seeder. I'd like more land, he says, spreading himself out in the kitchen chair. If I had two hundred acres, he says, I'd quit teaching school and farm.

Ions and ozone have no place here, nor does sporadic E, nitric oxides and particulate matter, NASA grants, proposals to NSF, rockets and space shuttles. What are all these to the cry of gulls over the field as he plows, the magpies chucking and strutting over the open porch, the cat's cry in the night and the answering owl?

Please forget it, she said, and just be my mother, here on this peaceful farm. All I need is a mother, she said. But she touched my hand with hers, slim and dark with memory and clenching it told me that if only she had been there, she would have strangled him for me herself, knifed him through and through. She would have crushed his head for me against the marble newel post.

* * *

Forget it. Forget I even mentioned it, huffs and puffs my uncle, the big bad wolf who came into my bedroom dressed in nothing but his grandmother's grin and a pair of red-ridinghood red and white striped pajama bottoms.

Alice has just recited a list of declarations of war and unprovoked invasions—amounting to more than anyone would ever believe, comments Aunt Lila—occurring inside of the last five years in Europe. Japan is now menacing our west coast, Alice points out to him. If Hitler conquers Britain, does my uncle think he would stop for a minute to engage in a pincer movement with his ally, Japan, before attacking our sacrosanct shores?

Forget it, forget I even mentioned it, my uncle says.

The rope has tightened around my uncle's neck and he has suspended himself, is dangling now, from the dining room chandelier. His blue eyes are bulging out of their sockets; the skin on his face is taut. His head leans over to the side as though he were listening to some distant sound, perhaps to a choir of angels.

A cigar is held tightly between the stiffened first and second fingers of his right hand and the ash falls lightly to the floor. His silver and onyx ring winks in the light of the chandelier which Aunt Lila has just turned on.

* * *

It's evening. The dishes have been cleared away. Alice and I did them, I washing and Alice drying. I'm sitting at the dining room table and putting together a puzzle which I received from my mother just before she went into the hospital. I have been working on it for several nights now, keeping it together on a large tray and putting it on top of the kitchen broom closet at bedtime.

The puzzle is a colored photograph of a castle set on the side of a long, sloping mountain. There is a grove of trees in the lower right-hand corner of the puzzle. I have it all finished except for the sky and parts of the grayish-brown turrets.

Aunt Lila is sitting by the radio where she can get light from the chandelier, embroidering the cutwork on a christening dress she is making for someone's grandchild, chewing her gum quietly with her mouth closed, which is the proper way to do it.

Music is coming from the radio; a woman is singing "Pennies From Heaven", an old song from many years ago. Mrs. Loop is sitting on the rocker across the room, eyes closed, her busy hands at rest for once and folded in her lap, rocking in time to the music. Alice is knitting my sweater, occasionally turning her head to look out the window at the gray night, lit up by a full moon. The dark shadows of the trees show up clearly against the sky. Soon Alice will only see herself reflected in the window as it grows darker and darker outside.

I have finished the last turret in my puzzle. It has a flag flying from the top. The sky I'm now filling in is intensely blue; the air is warm—it is midsummer. See how dark and lush the grass is and the leaves on the trees—see how green they are? The castle is in England on the northeast coast. On the grass beside the walls the sun is very hot, but inside, in the halls and large rooms of the castle, the air is cool, even cold, especially in the dungeons, of which there are three—one built below the other.

My uncle is lying down on the sofa against the west wall of the dining room, his head propped up by a pillow, reading a copy of *Popular Mechanics*. The singing has stopped on the radio and now a comedian is telling jokes. My uncle looks up from his magazine to listen and laughs abruptly at one of the jokes, then goes back to his reading.

I am in the castle. I stand at the end of a long stone hallway paved with flagstones. The walls are hung with red banners and broken at intervals by narrow slits . . . windows . . . that let in a dusky light. The banners are a dull red, almost magenta, dyed to that hue perhaps by the dimness.

In the distance are a group of people listening to a guide—they surround him in an uneven clump, looking up. Perhaps he's explaining to them the significance of the hangings, or perhaps he's defining the armorial bearings within the escutcheons that are embroidered on the heavy cloth in thin gold thread.

I peer into the other end of the hall to see my mother, or rather my daughter, who is part of the group. She is there—see?—in the light-colored sweater: a small person . . . or no . . . rather tall, tall and thin. I go to look out the window slit beside me, leaning my head far over to see the deep green grass on the hillside and the moat that encircles the castle. Then I look back, and . . . the hall is *empty!* Could the guide have taken the group farther ahead? I hurry to catch up, I break into a run, I race down the flagstones in terror. The hall is so long, you see, it appears to have no ending—only a kind of gloom in the distance that keeps moving ahead of me as I run. Where did they go, the people, the guide, my daughter? I try to scream, but I have no voice. I scream and scream and the hall echoes only with the hollow thud of my running feet.

It is a dream I have over and over again through all the years, and sometimes it's my daughter who is lost and sometimes it's my mother.

My uncle laughs again. That was a good one! he says. He laughs and laughs for a long time. Mrs. Loop smiles, her eyes still closed. My aunt's face is still; she is intent on her embroidery, she is lost in the beauty, the delicacy of it. It surrounds and encloses her.

Alice is looking out of the window, absently, the knitting needles and six inches of sweater lying in a heap in her lap. My uncle laughs again—a slow, drawn-out, appreciative laugh. He's what I call a real comedian, he says. He pulls a cigar from his shirt pocket and lights it, huffing and puffing, sending little balls and bunches of smoke out across the room. Mrs. Loop, who is still rocking with her eyes closed, says, please don't drop ashes on the sofa, dear.

Ashes! says my uncle. When did I ever drop ashes on the sofa? No one answers. My aunt holds the bodice of the christening dress away from her and looks at it critically. Half of it is finished: tiny crescents and leaf shapes stretch from the shoulder to the center front.

Alice is asleep in her wheelchair, her head hanging to the side, her loose mouth slightly open. She looks helpless and vulnerable. I forget the terrifying strength of her arms as I look at her; I forget the piercing clarity of her mind.

My aunt is rummaging in her sewing basket for her small scissors. Then, with them in hand, she very carefully cuts the tiny holes with the sharp tips. She is far away in a fairy land of white linen and silk thread, of black and cream and pink crepe pleats, of shirred bodices and ruches, of zippers set in perfectly, of hems which hang evenly all the way around. She loves to make beautiful things; she lives in a beautiful world, far away from the one in her second floor back apartment, far away from my uncle as he, on his side, lives far away from her.

* * *

The French cookbook has a stained cover; the *fleurs de lis* run in orderly columns down the white buckram spine. *Quiche,* Mrs. Loop murmurs to herself, General Information: the secret of turning out a good *quiche Lorraine* is baking it in the upper third of a preheated oven. She looks up, pursing the lips of her tiny mouth. Mrs. Loop has two ovens; one very large, the other much smaller. For the *quiche* she will use the smaller oven.

My mother cooked all of her married life on an oil range. The upper third of the oven burned everything on the top, the lower third burned everything on the bottom. She therefore baked all that she baked in the middle—both French and American. She was always talking of the day when she would have a nice new electric range, a day that never came.

It's 1940 and we have moved to Hudders Wharf. Our house faces the Delaware River. My mother and I go often to sit on the benches in front of the river wall and watch the ships go up and down, the big ones guided by tiny tugboats which have high, breathy whistles. My father lies very sick on the second floor of our house behind us, his strong body wasted away by chronic leukemia to less than one hundred pounds. He has come home from the hospital to die. When he dies my mother and I will go to live in Philadelphia with my aunt.

I lean over the riverwall and drop cinders into the water, making pricks in the water like the rain does. Anna! my mother says sharply. You'll fall in. She is holding her hands tightly together, rubbing the thumbs over each other, looking at me and frowning. Her heavy winter coat hangs on her loosely and her dark eyes are large and feverish. She will soon be dead herself of influenza.

* * *

Drifting through the euphoric haze of Elavil, I awake and see her sitting before me on the hospital chair, her knees stiff and held tightly together, her dark eyes riveted on mine—my daughter. The news had come—what was it?—that an old man had died, a man who was at one time my uncle. And then came the certainty in me that I had killed him, killed him at last.

But instead of the comfort I might have expected, I was filled with the horror of what I had done, that it had come, finally, to this. Dread dug in and took hold of me. How can I face them again—Aunt Lila, Alice, Mrs. Loop—who had in spite of everything loved this unlovable man? What would they say to me, what would they do?

Terror rose up in me relentlessly, I could see his broken head, I could hear his gasping, rasping breath, I could see his tongue lolling messily out of his mouth. I walked the floor and wrung my hands. Talk to me, I said to her, talk to me of your classes or about a book or a movie.

Alone with her, her father in South America on a research grant, unable to quell the horror that gripped me, I see with new eyes the living room walls, incredibly clear and bright. The mirror moves out toward me, the windows beg me to throw myself through them, my ears ring with screams of indictment. I have killed him over and over, I have ripped off all of his masks.

You exhibit a curious mixture of compassion and hate, the analyst says to me, opening the folder on his knee. I look at him through the white haze of the hospital room. You have had a sudden and violent attack, he says, a type of breakdown . . .

I look at him through the layers of time—this young man—and wonder how many have felt the lash of my tongue, how many like him have died from the bite of my teeth, from my traitorous lips? I am filled to the eyes with self-loathing, I have killed him over and over, in all of his masks, under all of his aliases.

I walk the living room floor with this nightmare. I clutch my head with disgust. Alarmed beyond thinking, my daughter runs to pound on the doctor's door down the road and I, maddened with fear by now, run to the bathroom for the Seconal bottle and take all the capsules at once.

In the office furnished with antiques and tropical plants, the analyst's eyes stray to the clock just out of my sight: my time is just about up—fifty minutes of fathomless probing, of finding the child within me, the mother who was lost too soon. What could he possibly know of all this, how much does he think I'll tell?

* * *

The snow is falling outside. Little balls of white spread over the back porch, covering it completely as I watch. The sky appears to be a white dome; the mountains are now invisible. The snow lies around the house and over the fields. The dragging footsteps of the geese break the snow cover here and there and a trail of small cat prints crisscross below the tree. The magpies leave spidery hieroglyphs all over as they twitch in random jumps to steal barley from the trough set out for the geese.

The cars creep along, down below on the snow-packed county road, making their way along its snaking length from the highway, around the hill on which perches our house, past the doctor's house, and across the valley.

The snow is thick on the ground; the porch has disappeared under it. The trees at the end of the yard are no longer there. The fence on the north end of the field has blended in with the general whiteness. The county road is gone.

I am alone in the peaceful house, alone in a blanketing whiteness. The fact that I am to blame for everything is unquestionable. I accept that fact and watch the snow, the greens of spring and summer, the leaves blowing by my window in the fall. I care only for the quiet, the quiet that descends as now, because above all things I am old, centuries upon centuries old.

The door is closed firmly, closed and locked against me. But I know she is in there, listening for footsteps, a signal heralding his return, or heralding the onslaught of fury from the others, of rage perhaps, or disgust.

The door is locked against me, yes, but the door is as old as I am, and I have the key. I grasp the knob and turn the key gently in the keyhole under it. I am very quiet for I don't want to frighten the little girl who sits so foolishly on the other side of the door.

I swing the door quietly inward. The little girl looks up, her brown eyes wide with fright and guilt. She is sitting on the side of the bathtub and holds a mirror in her hand. Her white cotton panties are lying in a heap on the chenille cover of the toilet. Her mother told her that ridiculous thing to save her from something that could possibly cripple her, and now she looks at me and her eyes are an accusation.

Will it never end, this spiral, this series of circles? What do we do to our daughters? What do we say to our mothers who confess their sins to us?

But then, what is so bad about it? It happens every day. It goes back to the Greeks, it goes back to the Sumerians, to the mound-builders. What woman alive is as pure as the snow outside my window? Do we not all hate and hate and pass it on as though a gift from Heaven?

I hold out my arms to the little girl. So what of it, Anna? And she comes to me in a mist of relief and peace, and I close her up in my arms. I melt her into myself.

VICTORIA

It was a Saturday morning in late November. Victoria was still on *Existentialism from Dostoevski to Sartre*, a text she'd vowed to get through before teaching began again in the fall. It was slow going, a slogging march, in fact, through a clutching undergrowth of philosophical flora. But she was not one to give up, and besides, she needed something to talk about that night. She must at least appear to understand Sartre. She shut the book with a dull thud and let her hand lie on the cover. She studied her hand—undersized and stringy, each finger lying in lonely isolation from its sister, the coral pink enamel dabbed on slits of nails bitten back to the quick.

So, she thought, according to Sartre the Anti-Semite finds identity by hating the Jews. Incredible. And how could such a subject lead to tenderness, even dalliance? Why did she get her mind set on Sartre for tonight, anyway?

"How do you feel about identity, Christopher? How do you feel about Sartre, about anti-Semitism?" *She speaks hesitantly, softly, smiling at the big blond sophomore in front of her—center fullback for the College soccer team—while she ices the petits fours for their dessert.*

But Christopher is too enamored to answer. He'd been watching the business with the cakes, devouring her with his eyes, longing to tell her what was in his heart but inhibited by their relationship . . . a student and his teacher . . . what would she think? Would she cut him dead? Would she freeze him into a block of ice? And of all the luck, for her to start on the subject of Sartre when all he wanted to speak of was . . .

"Is identity so important as all that, Christopher? Tell me what you think about it. Tell me . . ." *She finishes the last of the little cakes and lays the plate of them down in front of the boy, talking about Sartre, about anti-Semitism, about . . .*

No, no, no. It would never do, and Sartre had not opened up to her in any case. She must therefore skirt around the subject—the current one in Christopher's Philosophy 201 class—and let the boy freely explain it all: she the indulgent and considerate teacher, giving him that opportunity.

And if he wants to talk about something else . . .? If he wants to express some feeling he's had concerning her for so many weeks, so many months . . .?

But there now, the morning was moving along and the *filets de poissons* were still to be finished, her hair to be fixed and the dress picked up. She had already tried making the *roux*—twice. Hence the interlude with Sartre. It had been impossible to keep the stuff from scorching. Twice she'd scraped the brown butter and flour lumps into the sink—the last time whimpering a little. Now she felt strong enough to tackle the job again. There was no question—it had to be done: it was absolutely essential to the whole evening's maneuver.

Victoria walked over to the stove and the waiting saucepan. Compressing the thready line of her mouth, she melted the butter again, slowly. She blended in the flour, stirring with a fork, the whole of her meager body rigid with the expectation of failure. Just as the mass foamed and frothed together in viscous union, she snatched it off the burner and set it on the cool porcelain of the sink. An explosive exhalation of breath followed. Success! No brownish despair creeping up through the butter-white paste.

The poaching liquid bubbled now, on the second burner. As she poured, it hissed over the edge of the saucepan into the paste, clouding her glasses in a stinging haze of fish broth and vermouth. From the other counter Victoria took the half cup of milk and dumped it into the *mélange*. So far so good. Onto the heat again to stir and wait for the uncertain transition into the thick *velouté*. Victoria worked attentively, crisply businesslike about the thin mouth, the usual trace of bewilderment at the eyes and forehead.

Unbelievable that anyone would go to such trouble against such odds—that the visit from this boy would actually make it all worthwhile. One must be so excessively fussy. She slid her pale eyes sideways behind her glasses toward the despotic French cookbook, to the picture of Chef Jean on the front, peering at her intently, sure that she would botch it all. And yet she dared not flinch from him—there remained the business of the egg yolks and cream, and some show of grit was necessary since it could all so easily wind up in disaster. In went the egg yolks and cream.

Victoria crimped her eyes and drew a spoon through the sauce at exactly one minute after the boiling began. The spoon coated nicely—all the ingredients had blended miraculously into the elusive *parisienne.*

She was almost nonplussed: it worked out perfectly though Victoria had expected the usual failure. A good omen, perhaps.

Still, she could not accept all this need for care. She'd always wanted to be carefree, to do things lightly, casually and have them work out well. Or if they didn't, *peu importe!* But life for her was not so relaxed. She could never do anything easily—all was tension, disquiet.

And nothing ever worked out well. She couldn't even carry on a liaison—it was always spoiled by this fussily difficult job of cooking up the Encounter with just the right amounts of chance and surprise and submission so that the choice might never appear to fall to her, so that later they might ask each other, *How did it happen? How?*

Would he discover the other student was never invited? It was unlikely he'd ever find out, not knowing who the girl was. Yet it was still a worry. One must always strive to keep one's dignity, to remain free of implication in this sort of thing.

Victoria poured the smooth *parisienne* over the poached sole filets and sprinkled the whole with leathery, curling flakes of Swiss cheese. At the proper time she would run it under the broiler to brown. It had all worked out, and surely that was a good omen. And just the right thing to serve after all his talk of that summer tour of France with the International Club; of the *coq au vin* and the *croissants*—the babble that made him so appealing to her, brushing back his long pale hair at intervals, self-consciously playing the man of the world. It would be her joke; just enough of a spur to give her an edge, to make her years work for her instead of against. Yes, the *filets de poisson a la parisienne* tonight, and . . . perhaps . . . Sartre.

Still, she was not as carefree as she would have liked, and why this familiar defeatism? She had caught the boy's eye so often of late, and he was always in her office, talking her ear off. Did she instigate the thing? Why, the first time he'd smiled at her from down the hall she'd thought, *Don't flash your dimples at me, Christopher Atwood, looking for a grade.* But apparently that hadn't been his motive at all. The day before she'd arranged this dinner, he'd brushed her hand, and when she'd caught his gaze . . .

Victoria drew in her breath sharply. But that was very bad: *then of course he knows!* He'll know the other student was never supposed to come! Perhaps he knows already, is embarrassed by the whole thing, embarrassed and . . . perhaps . . . *repelled.* Victoria wrung her hands. Could that be? She glanced at Chef Jean, still watching her disdainfully. Sartre's Anti-Semite must have surveyed the Jews in much the same manner. Both Frenchmen seemed to unite in contemptuous scorn for her. Identity? Bah! She could not even cook a meal with nonchalance or understand the most fundamental ideas about Existentialism. And as for *affaires de coeur* . . . What a fool she'd been! Victoria quickly opened a drawer and swept the cookbook into it, aghast at the entire past week, the entire past year. She walked back to the chair pressing her hands tightly together.

Of course, it might not be like that at all. She knew her own natural capacity for expecting the worst and tried to jam the rising lump of despair back down her throat, willing herself to the easy openness that could anticipate the best. She decided not to think about it. He wanted to come, he even said he wanted to come. How else was she to interpret it? A devoted student, a devoted teacher—she had nothing to be ashamed of.

"We have nothing to be ashamed of, Victoria, nothing . . . do you hear? Do you understand?"

"Of course, Christopher. Really . . . it just . . . happened!"

"*And I'm so glad it happened, Victoria, I've never been so glad.*" *He reaches out to touch her hand, his eyes shining, his cheeks flushed, and the room dissolves around them, they're drowning in each other's eyes, literally dying with love, dead, buried . . . the ultimate existential experience—merging their two identities into the nothingness of the grave, Oh God!* Victoria clutched her head. What was she going to *talk* to him about?

The textbook, *Existentialism,* lay on the table. Inside its covers the Anti-Semite raged, fighting all his young life for an identity—a thing Victoria had never thought so important. It was emotion she was concerned with. M. Jean had an identity—chef *extraordinaire.* Ah, yes. But what good was that? Where was the emotion in his precise measurements and overbearing surveillance? Identity Victoria could do without. What she had searched for all *her* life was an authentic emotion. A real love, a real hate, free from doubts, questions, the agonies of anticipation.

"*Christopher, I've waited so long for someone who could sweep me away*

. . . who could awake in me that kind of . . . would could show me what . . ."

"Do you mean that I . . . ?"

"Ah, Christopher, if you only knew . . ."

Victoria glanced at the clock and came back to life with a thud. Time. Always pushing at her back. It was imperative that her hair be rinsed. The mess was offensive to her, darkening the cuticles around her nails in spite of plastic gloves. And yet she could not trust a salon—the meringue of hair they arranged on her head put ten years on the face underneath. They were oblivious to the fact that the young style called for masses of ringlets. And besides, salons were so public.

No, she must do it herself, and quickly, so she'd be able to get to Mortozzi's by four o'clock to pick up her dress. Her hair first, then. And afterward, her dress. A cup of tea at five o'clock to wind up with, to help put things into perspective. Her whole future didn't hinge on tonight; and besides, it might all come out beautifully. She must keep that thought firmly in mind.

Victoria slipped off her glasses and put them in their case behind the cups in the cupboard. Then she pulled the little Italian provincial chair under the doorbell on the living room wall, slipped off her scuffs, and stepped up on it to lift the bell cover and disconnect the wires. She abhorred being interrupted at certain times, and the operation with the rinse was one of them.

Assembling her materials in the bathroom she breathed easier; now there was no possibility of intrusion. The apartment door was locked, the bell disconnected, the phone turned down, covered with a thick towel and buried in the living room closet. The business with the hair must be done under cover, the result as though a miracle. *Voilà!* Ten years shed by the grace of l'Oréal. If anyone were to see her in the process—Heaven forbid! Head wrapped in plastic, dribbles of greenish brown insinuating themselves from beneath it, over the temples, behind the ears. Telling the world, betraying her secret. No, it must be done in private, and in peace.

And so to work in the security of her hermetic lair. First the plastic gloves, then the mix of color and fixative. Dribble the mess down the parted pieces of hair. Nasty smell. Mustn't get it in the eyes, adding blindness to everything else. Lift up the left wave. Behold: a row of white hairs, stark white—short and new—coming in crowds now, mobs. The Juggernaut of Time creeping inexorably over her scalp.

The creme rinse afterward and the hair wrapped tightly on curling rods, the head encapsulated in plastic, in pain, in torture. The effort it took to maintain a modicum of attractiveness and the effort it took to conceal the effort was almost more than Victoria could handle. And yet she did it year after year, as though for some definite purpose.

Thirty-five minutes passed beneath the cap of her dryer and the operation was complete. Victoria's newly darkened hair now framed her small, slightly bewildered face with a nimbus of corkscrew curls. The doorbell was carefully reconnected, the phone exhumed. She was ready now to pick up her dress at Mortozzi's, five blocks away on Granby Street.

* * *

The place was empty of customers. Racks of dresses, skirts, tapered pants, knickers, and blouses lined the walls, the folds hanging stark and lifeless from the gaunt plastic shoulders: El Greco paintings, size 5 to 18. Victoria looked around for Mr. Mortozzi. She felt almost safe in his hands. Whatever he suggested she felt she could wear with as little self-consciousness as was possible, for her. He knew just what should go with what, and she felt she could trust him. In fact, she looked upon him as a father. She thought he looked a little like her father just before he died. She trusted Mr. Mortozzi, yes. Almost entirely. The man appeared from behind the dressing room curtain at the back of the store and walked heavily toward her, smoothing back his white hair.

"Ah! Mrs. Threadman."

"Hello, Mr. Mortozzi." Victoria had stopped telling him that she was not married, that in fact she would much prefer he call her by her first name, or at the very least *Ms.* Threadman. She had made a little joke out of it, rehearsing her speeches beforehand in a grinding effort to make them appear impromptu. But it had been to no avail. He was of the old school after all; and he still asked now and then about her nonexistant husband.

Mr. Mortozzi stood before her expectantly, smiling with great good will.

"May I try on the dress?" she asked.

"The dress, of course." The man turned on the ball of one large foot and disappeared into a side room where the alterations were done. He returned holding the dress. It was a slim, straight plaid with blue predominating, a low V-neck, and a wide belt cutting it across the middle. The dress looked impossibly risqué now, and very scanty, especially draped over Mr. Mortozzi's massive arm, straining as usual against his blue worsted sleeve. A most unlikely man to be running a woman's boutique: a fit study for Michelangelo.

"Well," ventured Victoria. "What do you think?"

Mr. Mortozzi smiled wider and lifted his huge shoulders. "It's a dream of a dress," he said simply.

Victoria always marveled at his sincerity. There was nothing for it but to trust his judgement. "And shoes?" she asked.

"What do *you* think?" he said, and gestured like the Sistine God toward the tiny alcove of shoes across the store.

Victoria flushed with confusion at this tribute to her fashion sense, since to think with certainty about anything—except perhaps the Romantic period in France—was completely outside her province. "I had thought perhaps those slingback platforms on the table." Victoria hesitated. "But perhaps they're too high for me."

Mr. Mortozzi took her arm and steered her toward the alcove. "They're the newest thing," he said.

"They're young looking . . ."

Mr. Mortozzi nodded in agreement. "Yes," he said. His tone was completely sincere. Victoria felt slightly comforted. They were young looking, she reasoned; she was small and, from the back, very young looking. Why not? Why not, indeed! She took them—with much misgiving.

* * *

She'd decided to wear the dress home, the shoes, too—in case she should run into Christopher—and she carried her other things in Mortozzi boxes, tied with gold string. It would be well to look completely casual, as though she had just rushed home from shopping for this little affair. She must make sure, too, that she was convincingly distressed that the other student hadn't come, but not enough so to cancel the whole thing. She must strive to be disappointed, but delighted to make the best of it.

Of course, it would be a surprise to Victoria if it worked out at all. The truth is, one must always expect the worst. She peered anxiously down the street, myopic without her glasses which she never wore except when at home alone. She could see no one she knew. Her new wooden platforms thudded heavily on the sidewalk, measuring as they did some five inches high at the heel. They felt enormous at the end of her weedy legs and the word "conspicuous" kept creeping into her consciousness. If one expects the worst, she thought, approaching complete misery, one will always be happily surprised if it doesn't occur.

Victoria was tired by the time she reached the fourth floor of her apartment house, and her feet and legs ached from her stilt-like shoes. She had been tense all day and would have welcomed a nap. But her trip to Mortozzi's had taken longer than she'd expected and it was already five-thirty; only an hour left to make the salad and ice the petits fours before the appointed time: six-thirty. Stiff with anxiety, she turned the key in the lock and opened the door. The whole scheme was becoming too difficult to pull off.

In the kitchen she swept *Existentialism* from the table top and dumped it in the drawer beside Chef Jean. She felt compassion for the Anti-Semite whom she saw as distressingly misled. Rather than identity, he needed a good passionate Encounter, an authentic emotion to fill up his empty insides. Madame Bovary, now, was not misled. She was indiscreet, yes; but she knew what she was missing. Victoria could understand Emma Bovary, and wanted the same thing she'd wanted—but without her indiscretion, of course, with its disastrous implication. Yet this yearning for the grand emotion was, Victoria thought, her problem. She could lecture intelligently on the unfulfilled French Romantics, could analyze all the dynamics of their passions which she understood completely, could explain them all unerringly to her students, and yet she could never experience them. Victoria: the unfulfilled Romantic—there is no Encounter without great risks, apparently.

"What risks?" he whispers, his lips close to her hair. She feels his breath on her cheek, feels lightheaded, giddy, faint. Could this be It? Could this be her Grand Encounter?

"Christopher, no . . . this is not for us . . . you're too young . . . and I . . . I. . . ."

"We can go away, we can go to France, we can leave next week . . ."
"No, Christopher, no . . ."
". . . yes, to France. I have some money . . . an inheritance . . . my father . . . an aunt . . . she raised me . . . or rather, a grandmother . . . my father's

mother . . . she left me some bonds . . ."

Victoria sighed and glanced at the clock. Time was moving along: she must time things carefully, she must be icing the petits fours when he arrives, must look pleasantly rushed. She slipped off her shoes and placed them at the door of the kitchenette, ready to slip into when the bell rang, and began tearing up lettuce for the salad. She could picture Christopher hurrying toward the apartment house door, perhaps taking the stairs in preference to the slow elevator, his pale hair lifting with every step.

Victoria finished the salad and began setting the table. Her shoulders ached. She pulled her neck down and hunched over. Her whole body was tensed for the ringing of the bell—no wonder her shoulders ached. This will never do, she must relax. She took down a cup and saucer and deliberated between making a cup of tea and icing the cakes. Precious minutes wasted. She decided to ice the petits fours, suddenly realizing that she could never do it properly with the boy looking on. She must be just finishing up when the bell rings. She took the powdered sugar and mixer out of the cupboard and, trembling with the need for haste, hurriedly made the runny icing to pour over the small squares of cake and the thicker, colored paste to use in the tube for the flowers. But when she got to the last step—that of squeezing out the green icing into tiny leaves—it dawned on her that she had been working a long time. Sick with anxiety, she twisted her stiffened neck around to look at the clock.

It was six forty-five.

Victoria's face drained of expression. Fifteen minutes late. Of course, it was just what she'd expected, and it surely meant that he'd grasped the significance of the thing and elected to slip out of an awkward situation. She had certainly not been discreet enough this time. But then she must keep a tight hold on herself. He might come at any minute, breathless with running. It would never do to appear upset. At seven o'clock, Victoria decided she'd give him up.

She busied herself with making a cup of tea, hurrying still with an urgency she couldn't shake off. The kettle was full on the burner and she took a lemon from the refrigerator. Of course there was no harm done, she reasoned, except between the two of them. There would be a strain between them but she could be very cool about it. It was not the first time a student misunderstood simple academic interest for something else. A sudden coldness gripped her—unless he told some of his fraternity brothers. She stood stock still. *That* would be awkward—it would be all over campus by Monday. The kettle was steaming. She poured the hot water over the tea bag and dropped in a wedge of lemon, her arm trembling clear up to the shoulder. How could she lecture Monday on Baudelaire, fearful that the back row was snickering at her? Fearful only because she could never see the back row clearly without her glasses. She was in despair. But how could she blame the boy for something she could only imagine he'd done? She pulled the tea bag out of the cup and dropped it in the sink.

Then a sudden thought struck her: had she really been clear about this affair tonight? She groped back to their talk in the office and wondered if she'd really got the invitation out in the open. In her eagerness to be discreet, perhaps she'd been cryptic. Perhaps the boy was still wondering what she'd been driving at, or perhaps he just took it all for maundering. She dragged every word of the interview with Christopher painfully and foggily to the surface and could come to no conclusion. Then she glanced at the clock: five after seven.

Victoria slumped against the counter. Oh, to hell with it all. Her mind emptied—the gestures, the sighs, the touches, the half-formed phrases of lovers, they all spilled out, vanished. A few minutes later she pushed herself away and went through the ritual of disconnecting the bell, locking the door, burying the telephone. Never had her abhorrence of possible intrusion been so acute as it was at that point. Yet those who came to her door and went away disappointed during these lockouts never made themselves known to her later, nor did those who dialed and heard the phone ringing ineffectually ever ask her what she had been up to on such and such a day.

But that was of no concern to her, sitting now at her table in the half-light of temporary hibernation, thinking—almost peacefully—of permanent hibernation. Better yet, complete obliteration. What escaped her was a way to do it discreetly. That is, a way to evaporate gradually into thin air without the mess (for instance) and the scandal (especially) that a suicide leaves behind.

She sat at her table for a long time with the cup of tea before her, fragrant with its slice of lemon, and thought it all over. Sat, in fact, until her tea had grown quite cold.

THE VICTIM

He was standing a block away by the empty candy store lighting a cigarette. No, not a cigarette. It was a cigar, a long, thin cigar. Laura remembered it quite clearly. The street lamp had just turned on in front of her house but the candy store was in shadow. He was shielding the match flame with his left hand while his right hand held the match cover and the lighted match. She could see the flame brighten his face—his cheekbone, a high cheekbone, and his ear. They were both reflecting a vivid red from the flame.

A Judy Collins record was playing downstairs. It was a new record she had just bought and she was playing it over and over again. She had heard the screams over the fiddle and guitar section in the "Fishermen Song", but supposed them to be the screams of children, playing in the park. No, they were leaving the park, chasing her under the trees, laughing and screaming, having fun, chasing her all the way home. It had happened every day for a long time, after her father had stopped coming to see her. How long had it been? She couldn't remember. Her mother had said they were just having fun, that she should have joined them. What was the matter with her, anyway, that she could never have any fun?

Later that night, Barry leaned toward her in the silent living room with a match to light her cigarette. He was grinning at her—it was a lopsided grin that showed his white, even teeth. She said she would rather have one of his cigars instead. He shook out the match and threw it into the fireplace and then put his hand into the inside pocket of his jacket. He had a gun there, the outline was unmistakable.

They had found the woman, an old woman, on the sidewalk under the east window of the candy store. There were bruises on her arm and a bullet had blown off part of her scalp. They found the piece of scalp five feet away, in the gutter. The woman had been robbed. They found her purse dumped upside down on the sidewalk and the wallet empty. But Laura didn't hear about the incident until the next morning. She thought the screams were from children playing in the park.

What she wanted to remember were the facts. They would be sure to insist on the facts, and hers was the only private house within two blocks. If she were really to turn him in, she might well be the only witness.

* * *

She had met Barry outside the RCA building the month before. He looked very tall and impeccable in his light trench coat. She was impressed at once with his high cheekbones, the way his tanned skin was pulled so tightly over them, and with his wide, laughing mouth. Later on he gave her one of his long, thin cigars to smoke and lit it for her. She wouldn't inhale, though, and he laughed and laughed about it as though it were a terrific joke. It was an unrestrained laugh, with a flattening out at the end, a laugh that sounded like a schoolboy having fun.

She intended to call the police while he was sleeping, the bedroom being on the second floor, but she was afraid he might waken and hear her. And besides, was he really the one?

So instead, she was very quiet and sat at the window looking out in order not to disturb him, in order not to disturb anyone, but especially her mother, for fear it might provoke her into forbidding her trip that night with her father. Her mother had not liked the way she was dressed in any case, and was in a very bad humor—why was it that fitted dresses looked so bad on her? Why was it that she had no hips to speak of? Why was she so set on going, anyway, as though there were no one else in the world who mattered to her besides her father?

It had seemed foolish to her mother that Laura would sit so long, waiting for her father to come from Norristown to take her to the carnival, a father who was so thoughtless, so mean. But once when Laura herself, in a frenzy of utter heartbreak, called her father thoughtless and mean, her mother slapped her and sent her to her room.

Perhaps she could let the Collins record play while she called. She could let it play on the dining room turntable which stood by the steps to the second floor, and call on the kitchen phone under cover of the music. If Barry came down and surprised her anyway, she could pretend to be talking to her mother at the nursing home.

She must be careful, though, in how she did this. It had become more and more difficult to talk to her mother on the phone because of the way in which she had begun rambling and the things she kept remembering, accusing Laura of loving her father, for instance, or of not loving him. And Barry knew all about this problem.

Her mother had asked her what in the world she was waiting at the window for. Her father wasn't coming that week, hadn't she made that clear to Laura? He had called that morning, she said, to tell her that he was going to New York on business.

* * *

Barry was the first man to have taken Laura to bed, and she couldn't imagine what he saw in her to attract him—he himself was so good looking, so tall, so neat and smart in his clothes, in his trench coat, in his brown denim suit, in his square-toed Wellington boots. She had wondered about it for weeks, and yet it had all seemed quite legitimate. He had seemed genuinely amused by her.

He had given her his package of long cigars and taken her to Stouffer's to dinner. There were mirrors everywhere. She could see his reflection in them, just the back of his head and his high cheekbone and his ear. She didn't look at herself.

He had said he was coming to see her Friday night and that he would bring some live crabs and white wine for dinner. He said it would be fun, it would be amusing to him and, of course, to her.

But it got later and later Friday, and she wondered why he was taking so long. She went up to the second floor of her little house, her mother's house, to look out the bedroom window to where the candy store stood and saw the man by the darkened store window. He was holding his left hand up, shielding the flame from the match so it would not blow out, trying to light his long cigar. But she could not see his face, or even his body which was in shadow—just part of his cheekbone and his ear, reflecting a vivid red from the flame of the match.

Laura had stayed at the window waiting until it became quite dark and she fell asleep. Her mother had shaken her and told her she absolutely had to go up to bed, that her father was not coming, as she very well knew. Her mother had been crying because Laura was acting as though there were no one else in the world who mattered to her but her father. So Laura went up to her bedroom, her eyes scratchy and tight in their sockets. Her chest ached each time she breathed.

Barry patted Laura on her shoulder and grinned, telling her that of course it wasn't her fault, her mother was a selfish bitch and Laura had been her victim all along. But he thought the story was really very funny and laughed a long time to himself.

When Laura went back on the day shift, Barry came every day to take her out to lunch. She never found out where he worked. He said that what he did was "classified" so she supposed him to be with the FBI or CIA, since he surely looked the part. But now she must get all the facts straight in her mind and decide whether or not to call the policeman.

She saw the brown spots on his coat—three small spots about as big around as the end of a pencil eraser—when he had come in the night before holding the green-glass bottle of white wine. The spots were at the hem of his coat, in the front. He said a car splashed him on Market Street and he soaked the edge of his coat in cold water in her bathroom. By the time dinner was ready, the spots had soaked out and he hung the coat on her shower rack to dry.

She and Barry went to bed early. She felt giddy from the wine and had trouble getting up the steps. He insisted she try another cigar but she still wouldn't inhale as he suggested. She sat on the edge of the bed and filled her mouth with smoke and then blew it out, laughing a little to herself. Barry kept looking at her intently, his head thrust a bit forward, his hands in his pockets. Then he called her little lonely Laura, and turned on his heel away from her.

Perhaps he should move in with her, Barry had said while they lay together later in the darkened room. It was a lonely neighborhood, he said, and Laura should have a man to protect her. He could take her places, too, so she could have a little fun. She never seemed to have any fun, he said. Why was that? he wondered. He propped himself up on one elbow and looked at her, frowning darkly. Did she have something against having fun? Then he threw himself back down on the bed and laughed and laughed, telling Laura that her mother had surely been a neurotic bitch.

The carnival used to come to her neighborhood every Fourth of July. Her father was to have taken her there but he went to New York on business instead, and she never saw him again. Her mother said he had married. The woman he married had four young girls of her own and now he was their father.

The old woman who was shot was a prostitute, the policeman told her, still active in her trade at sixty-five. She had been wearing three sets of false eyelashes when they found her and her fingernails and toenails were painted silver. Why should she bother to get involved, thought Laura, with such a sordid person? The old woman had been wearing a red sequinned dress with a very short skirt, and she was carrying at least two hundred dollars in her wallet. The police had contacted the young man who lived with her—her grandson, so the young man said. And he told them that she was carrying at least two hundred dollars.

Barry's wallet had been bulging with money. Laura saw his reflection in the darkened kitchen window as she stood washing the crabs in the sink. He was at the kitchen door behind her, arranging the money in his wallet, smoothing the bills and straightening them out.

The old woman's head was covered with blood and part of her scalp was blown away. The policeman told Laura about it at the door that morning, and Laura knew he was trying to scare her. He could see the skull, he said, of the victim. They supposed her to be carrying approximately two hundred dollars.

Laura had found a sequin that morning on the kitchen floor, a red sequin, near the place where Barry stood the night before when he was arranging his money.

But Laura told the policeman that she had heard nothing. She had been playing records all evening with the volume turned up, and heard nothing. It was done, the policeman said, with a thirty-eight caliber hand gun, a gun that could fit easily into an inside coat pocket. It was entirely possible, he said, that the gun had a silencer on it. They had amassed a great deal of information on the suspect, he said, since this appeared to be the sixth in a series of similar crimes: the shooting and robbing of old women.

* * *

Laura wrote a long letter to her father when she found his address three years after he married and moved to New York, but he never answered it. He had his hands full, her mother had told her, dealing with four young girls. It seemed they were all very attractive.

Never mind, said Barry, grinning at her and patting her on the shoulder. Your mother, he said, was a spiteful bitch.

Barry had noticed Laura as she left the RCA building after the late shift, though he had frightened her, walking up behind her so quietly in the dark parking lot and grasping her arm that held her large purse. She had surprised him, he told her later. He hadn't realized she was so young, and all he had really wanted from her were directions to a drug store. He was also surprised, he said, that she had been so attractive. From a distance, she certainly hadn't looked attractive.

Laura was standing in her room on the day her father was to come, looking at herself in the dresser mirror. The fitted dress she was wearing had been bought by her father on their last outing together. Her father liked the dress and so she had insisted on wearing it even though her mother disliked the way it hung so loosely on her, crying out, so to speak, for a belt to give it some shape.

Barry said flatly that Laura's mother was obviously a spiteful bitch and not just unhappy as Laura insisted was the case. She also sounded like a miser, he said, a type who liked to hide things away for herself. He was interested in old women who hid things, he said. He had read many books on the subject. Sometimes they hide things in the cellar, for instance, or in the spaces below the kitchen cupboards. Sometimes they carry all the money they own around with them in large, black bags.

Barry searched the cellar of Laura's house and took all the cupboard bottoms apart in the kitchen, but he was unable to find anything. Yes, Barry said, Laura's mother was indeed a spiteful bitch, but he was sure he'd find her cache in the house somewhere.

Laura walked into the kitchen and picked up the telephone receiver which shook in her hand. She would call; yes, she would call. "The Fishermen Song" was playing on the turntable in the dining room. The fiddles and guitars sang and trembled on the air, Judy Collins' voice, gentle and lazy, drifted into the kitchen. Laura's eyes stung and also her chest ached as if she had been crying for a long time.

Her mother had told her that it was foolish of her to cry over such a heartless man, although he had been a good father, Heaven forbid that Laura should say she didn't have a good father. But now he was married with four young girls to bring up, all very attractive.

Laura dialed the number the policeman gave her. The policeman's name was Morgan and he was looking for facts so that they could clear things up, once and for all. An unsolved murder was a dangerous thing, Morgan had told her, looking steadily into her eyes. Since her house was the only private residence for several blocks, perhaps the next victim might be Laura herself.

If Barry came down after she got Morgan on the phone, Laura thought, she could pretend to be talking to her mother. Morgan would understand, if she had time to identify herself. The number rang once at the other end and the voice of the desk sergeant answered. Laura asked for Morgan. "Morgan," she said quietly. If Barry came down and surprised her, she would pretend to be telling her mother about Barry, about perhaps her wedding with Barry. She smiled slightly to herself.

A voice came on, Morgan's voice. Laura recognized it immediately. "Hello," the voice said. Then she looked up at the kitchen doorway. Barry was leaning against the door jamb, looking at her fixedly, the irises of his eyes very small and black. "Hello," she said into the receiver, and, as though speaking to her mother, added, "This is Laura."

Barry continued to look at her, breaking slowly into his lopsided smile. He reached into his pocket and then began flipping over and over in his hand what he had drawn out—a thirty-eight caliber pistol. It had a silencer on the end. "The Fishermen Song" was still playing in the dining room but Laura could hear clearly the pistol slapping against Barry's palm.

She smiled slightly at him, looking directly into his eyes. There comes a time, she thought, when one must stop playing the role of victim. "Mother," she said into the receiver, "you must try to get your nurse to bring you here right away . . ."

THE BUS RIDE

There is nothing so hot as August in Philadelphia, but the show windows in Gimbel's Department Store are all air conditioned and the manikins in them are dressed in fall woolens. Whip thin, in Zorro capes and tapered pants, they telegraph to the commonplace an unreachable female elegance.

Martha looks at them through her winged glasses. She's sitting in the number 42 bus that has been stopped dead in front of Gimbel's for a full five minutes. She's checked the delay with her watch. Every minute, another look.

One of the manikins in the window is a male, a young man. He sits at a small white table; fall leaves are scattered around his high-heeled shoes. He wears a suede jacket, no fringe, and looks up expectantly at the woman standing across from him. With her plaid cape slung back over her shoulder, she offers him a toasted cheese sandwich. A toasted cheese sandwich on a small white plate.

Martha stares at the plate. The sandwich on it, innocuous looking enough, is nevertheless heavily laced with strychnine. Urgency has darkened the young woman's painted blue eyes. Hurry and eat it, you fool, she is thinking, you hanger-on, you bastard. I must be off and leaving you. I must be packed and going before I suffocate in this crumbling hole of a house.

The bus sighs explosively but doesn't move. Martha sighs, too, and shifts in her seat. She wants to get home to Hudders Wharf on the New Jersey side of the Delaware, where her kitchen captures the breeze that comes with the evening tide; where the smell of the wild roses encloses the house like a cup in the spring; where her brother, Carl, waits impatiently for his Gorgonzola cheese.

Martha holds the package of cheese in her ample lap, along with three used books from Leary's and a round, flat box of rat poison.

The bus is crowded and smells like tomato soup and roasted

peanuts. At the opposite end of Gimbel's show window, three plaster students swing their mid-calf skirts as they turn to look at the young man and woman at the small table behind them. He's reaching for his sandwich, a satisfied smile painted on his smooth, complacent face. Ha. Little does he know what's in it for him; the searing blast of pain up the back of the neck and into the eyeballs, the legs turning leaden, the hideous convulsions on the floor.

The bus jerks to life and creeps forward to Gimbel's next window. Three young women stand there on a makeshift hill which is painted dusty brown and poked all over with tufts of dry grass, bending in a nonexistant wind.

Martha remembered it often. It happened in late summer, perhaps forty-five years before, when she was very little. She stood in the wind on the dry and tufty lawn where it sloped up to the house from the iron fence. The poplars ringing the house outside the fence whipped menacingly above her. She could see them reflected onto the long glass windows so clearly that they looked like they were bending and blowing and thrashing about right inside the house. And she was suddenly afraid because of something she had done that morning.

She ran to her mother and grandmother who were picking dead blossoms off the rose bushes and she confided to them in a trembling voice that there were trees inside the house and that Carl, her baby brother, asleep on the second floor, would be knocked out of his crib because they were whipping back and forth up there in the wind.

And they laughed and laughed at this latest bit of silliness from their little girl until they heard, loud and clear in the garden, the boy's screams from the open second story window.

Among the tufts of grass in Gimbel's window, two of the women stand poised, ready to run up their make-believe hill in the soft leather boots they are wearing—laced clear up to the knee. One wears a large, floppy hat, a scarf around her waist, and a skirt, brass-buttoned down to her calf. She looks like Martha's grandmother did, running up to Burlington Street for the doctor, wearing her garden hat, her skirt brushing the tops of her old-fashioned, high-topped shoes.

Little Martha stood at the upstairs window watching her go, her eyes feeling wide in her head, while her mother behind her cradled the screaming, outraged boy in her lap. He had fallen out of his crib in a tangle of arms and legs and mosquito netting, the side let down that morning by his sister who just wanted to see what would happen.

One of the manikins looks out the show window at Martha and she looks passively back at it through the pink plastic, silver-tipped frames of her glasses.

Martha, Martha, her mother had moaned, you've killed your baby brother. But Martha could clearly see that Carl was still very much alive, and she slipped from his bedroom, disgusted, to go into the garden and hide behind the lilacs on the river side of the house.

The bus wheezed and rumbled in the heat and Martha thought of the garden: the way it had elbowed its way over the years from the iron fence to the porch, shinnying its way up the railing and posts, trying to suffocate Martha while she slept. She thought of the wild roses bristling all over the lawn, gobbling up everything like pigs, locking Martha and Carl together inside their grandmother's cream-colored, wood-carved, turreted, musty old house.

The bus moved forward and blew to a weary stop at a red light on Gimbel's corner. The face of a young, dark-haired woman smiled knowingly from a poster at Martha. "Write that exciting news," she said, "on Chateau Royale Stationery." Martha is unimpressed; she prefers white bond, lined with blue ink, and glued together into a six-by-nine pad.

> *Dear Irene,*
> *I slept with a young man last week who stopped to admire Grandmother's roses. They all wear blue jeans these days, you know, with no underwear beneath. . .*

One of these young men stopped on the sidewalk by Martha's bus window, pushed a hand into the small front pocket of his tightly fitting blue jeans, and looking intently at the change he'd extracted. He was wearing pale, shoulder length hair, thongs, and a fringed jacket over a bare chest. An iron cross hung from his neck.

Martha stared at him and thought, they all look alike these days.

The young man walked forward to the bus door and it opened for him, politely. He boarded the bus, dropped his money in the box, and walked past Martha toward the back seats, ignoring her completely.

His chest had been golden-tan and smooth and he had lain with her at night on the grass by the river, the heavy smell of wild roses covering them like a cup as they rocked together, rocked toward the exquisite ending, when the blood sweeps into the ears and behind the eyes and the earth heaves itself out of its fruitless, dead-end orbit.

But that was a long time ago, when Martha weighed 112 and still played tennis. And before the wild roses sprung up like thistles all over her soft mattress of grass.

He would be fifty by now, a teacher some place, or perhaps a CPA like his father. His smooth chest would be tufted with colorless hair, his head perhaps bald, intent on his newspaper in the back of some crowded bus. At home after supper he'd go to bed to sleep on his back and snore. Years of ambition, bills, tonsillectomies, paranoia at promotion time, painting the bathroom walls, pouring cement for the new family room, sweating out the refinancing—all of it drying up the source. No longer interested in lying on a mattress of grass by the river. He would be fifty now, stuffed inside with lumpy, yellowing dough.

Back in Gimbel's window the young woman will hand the man across from her a sandwich for the next three weeks; but to Martha he is already dead, sitting with one elbow on the table, twisted in surprise and consternation toward her. He's tasted the bitter strychnine and already can feel the numbness in his arms and neck. He cannot believe she'd do it. His eyes are wide, the pupils dilated and very dark. They appear to fill up his eyes completely, like tiny black glass mirrors, glinting in the sun.

Martha can see herself reflected in them and she's running as though for her life, small legs running beneath a smocked yellow dress which is ballooning out in the wind, running up the sloping lawn, leading the others who have just heard her baby brother's cries, screaming herself along with him, making a great show for everyone.

The side had been left down on his crib, and of course, he had fallen out of it onto the hard tiled floor, tangled in mosquito netting and the ribbons of his nightgown. One of the ribbons was wound tightly around his neck.

Martha hadn't expected him to scream so loudly. She thought he would just fall out on his head, quietly.

> Dear Irene,
> I must tell you the latest tragedy, pulled by you-know-who. What has he done but shot himself with the handgun I gave him last Christmas. Anything to get attention.

He was sorry, very sorry—he hadn't really wanted to die just then. But Martha refused to meet his painted, pleading eyes nor look at herself reflected in their glassy mirrors. He had intended a flesh wound but the kick of the gun turned the bullet inward. He was sorry and could she do something about it?

Ha. It was too late. The shooting was much more permanent than the heart attack to which he resorted only the week before.

The bus gunned its motor impatiently, waiting for the light to turn green. Cars and buses and trucks and motorbikes streamed across Market Street, pouring endlessly from a prolific source somewhere in the heart of the city. The smell of roasted peanuts gave way to the odor of wild roses drifting heavily through the kitchen window, enveloping them both in its fragrance. He has already stiffened in that awkward position, still looking at her in surprise, and she knows she must go for the doctor first, before she unpacks from her trip to Mexico. How unfortunate that it happened while she was away and unable to watch what he was eating!

The doctor will admonish her about her carelessness: one must not leave rat poison, loaded as it is with strychnine, in the kitchen cupboard. Especially if one is leaving on an extended trip to Mexico and can't watch out for accidents. It isn't true as he insinuates that she did it on purpose. The little round can was rusted on the bottom and the salt shaker was right there for her to transfer the remainder of the rat poison into. She couldn't explain how it wound up on the shelf beside the pepper.

> Dear Irene,
> They say that men reach their sexual peak at nineteen and go downhill thereafter, while women reach theirs between thirty-five and forty-five. I read that in a book I bought today at Leary's.

And Martha remembered how the water lapped softly against the stones in the river wall as she leaned over the railing beside him, listening to his talk about the ships, about school, about men and women and when they reach their sexual peaks. They watched the water moving under them, down the wall toward Powell Street. The tide was going out. A ribbon of oil film gleamed blue and green on the dark water. A dead fish bumped along the wall, bobbing alone in the watery hollows, slipping into the oil slick and into the shadows of their heads which were close together, looking down into the deep, quiet water.

But she hadn't pushed him in and she told them over and over again that he toddled to the edge all by himself and then fell over the side in a tangle of mosquito netting and ribbons. She couldn't explain how the ribbon became so tightly wound around his neck. The tide was going out and all the neighbors and the firemen rushed to the scene and were looking for him down by Powell Street.

Martha, Martha, her mother moaned by the river wall, you've killed your baby brother. But how could she do such a thing, the neighbors said over and over to her mother. After all, Martha is only three years old.

Martha is twenty-three years old, or perhaps forty-three and the river breeze is warm and heavy as it brushes her side. She is walking furtively down the dusty, rutted path in front of the river wall, walking secretly to the young man's room in the Marina Lodge, the breeze carrying the smell of the wild roses which wrapped her in isolation for so long behind the iron fence in her grandmother's faded, musty old house.

The last traffic light turns green, the bus jerks again to life, and as though finally freed from racking torment, speeds up to a rumbling, headlong charge toward the Delaware River Bridge. Dilapidated store fronts on Sixth Street skim back toward Gimbel's as do the telephone poles and the struts of the suspension cables over the river.

Martha settles, relieved, against the hot, sticky back of her bus seat and looks at her watch. In twenty minutes she'll be home, away from the tomato soup of the Campbell's Soup factory in Camden, away from the roasted peanuts and iron crosses.

And it was not so bad as she had expected: the knife had penetrated cleanly and most of the bleeding must have occurred inside. She must hurry to be out of the house and on the way to Mexico, as innocent as a three-year-old, when they discover him. It was obvious he had done it himself because of the direction in which the knife was sticking in his chest.

    She stood with her back before the west window in the kitchen and the sun coming through it formed a halo around her dark hair, softening the subtle streaks of grey. Her glasses were hidden behind the cups in the cupboard. It was many weeks later, after the funeral, after she had lost thirty-five pounds, and after she had the A & B Gardeners clear out the wild roses and reseed the lawn. She smiled gently at the young man sitting in the kitchen chair, his elbows resting on his gold-tanned knees. He was looking up at her, his young eyes dark and touchingly serious. Barriers were erased between them, age was forgotten in one warm, swirling oblivion. She felt faint from the sight of his smooth, golden chest, the swell of his thighs, faint from the wash of heat over her, the tumid ache deep inside. The room dissolved, the young man dissolved, the world dissolved. The bus rumbled on.

    Martha's brother was waiting for her in the kitchen by the small white table when she finally got home, and his pleading look filled her stomach tightly with cold satisfaction. He pulled his left arm quickly to his side when he saw her and grabbed the leg of the table as he slid to the floor, his fingernails scraping the white paint on the metal leg. Carl, she said, exasperated, what have you done now?

    He tightened his hand like a claw on her arm as she bent over him, frowning, and he begged her not to call the doctor, saying that he had shot himself. Or perhaps he had used the knife. Or perhaps he had tasted the strychnine sprinkled on the cheese and was just now feeling the effects—the pain, the numbness, the uncontrollable nausea, the onset of the first convulsive fit.

    He held onto her arm for an hour after she helped him up and washed the long gash or hole or whatever it was in or on his chest. And after she settled him on the sunporch, arranging him as close to the edge as possible, four red lines stood out on her arm and turned a bluish green as the week went by.

    Would he stiffen there as rigor mortis set in? Would he scream and cry and thrash about in the baby blanket she had tucked around him? Or would he just fall out of bed and die, quietly? He should certainly do something, especially since he was no longer fit to teach senior math at the high school (that's what Irene had said) and only forty-five years old last February. Now they had only her annuity to live on. On top of that he's stopped helping her with the housework and the garden, too, because of his alleged heart attack.

Martha blinked back the scalding tears, welling up behind her glasses. She was on the very edge of panic. I need someone to talk to, she thought. A lump swelled and filled the base of Martha's throat: the roses needed clearing out and the windows needed washing and Carl would be spread out all over the kitchen table when she got back, correcting papers and in a spiteful mood because he hated to teach summer school, it being mostly reruns of algebra, trigonometry and geometry, and therefore bristling with the bad vibes of disgusted winter flunkouts.

Perhaps she could try 2-4-D on the roses. Perhaps Carl would be hit by a car tomorrow. Perhaps she could shoot him tonight with his hand gun or throw him into the river at high tide. Perhaps she could throw herself in after him.

The bus was approaching Martha's stop. She pulled up her matronly figure, confined discreetly in a lavender double-knit pants suit, and made her way carefully up the aisle to the front of the bus, holding her packages in one arm while she steadied herself with her other hand on the backs of the seats.

The young man in blue jeans watched her from the back of the bus. His bare, golden chest heaved a bit under his fringed leather jacket and iron cross. My God, he thought, lavender pants.

> ". . . amid the rubble were found the remains of an elderly woman."

There was a deadness inside her, close to disdain, when she thought of people who had slighted her in some way or who had done something stupid. She had just recently become aware of it, though it must have been present, that numbness, for some time. It was so surprising.

There was also fear, an abiding, low-grade fear that cramped and diminished her—a fear of eyes, of poking and prying among her things, and of the ridicule that would most certainly follow.

Her insides, those once-tender parts that had been so easily bruised, even torn, ripped to shreds at times, vulnerable until almost yesterday, her soft insides now felt cold and hard, like stone or wood. She dismissed everyone. She held everyone in contempt.

It was as though her core had hardened in direct proportion to the sagging and softening of her outer shell. She sighed again and again and the sighs came up from enormous depths, from the hardness buried deep inside her.

She was an old woman. It was hardly fair—to have lived so long, aware of everything, suffering and pain, and joy too, to have been sensitive for so long, kind, empathic, and now to feel so dull and apathetic, wasted by suspicion, locking everyone out, drawing the drapes, crouching distrustfully among the cushions of her Morris chair in the dark cave of her two-room apartment.

She had not always been this way. She could remember standing at the window in the large, airy house she had lived in for all of her married life, watching with rapture the wakening day, watching, for instance, the winter mist lifting slowly from the valley floor to reveal first the city, then the foothills, and then the mountains with the deep pink sun installed behind their peaks as though the spectacle were put on for her pleasure alone. She could remember walks in the delicate aspen forest not far from her home when the fragrance and gentleness of the breeze that touched her cheek was enough to make her fairly cry out with joy. She could remember when every hour, it seemed, was an occasion for celebration.

She could remember, too, an acute sense of self-sufficiency and security, when solitary trips to the other side of the world meant nothing to her. But she still had Edward to come home to in those days or to meet in some exotic place for a week's or a month's holiday. It was easy then to be self-sufficient and secure when she knew in the last analysis, if her luggage were to be lost in the Middle East somewhere, if her entire cache of traveler's checks were to be stolen, if she were to be struck down with dysentery in Mendoza, that Edward would be available to initiate a search from his end, to send supplementary funds, to arrange for her trip back to convalesce, to, above all, offer unwavering love and sympathy. It becomes very much like the difference between walking a tightrope above a safety net and walking one without—one's feet are so much surer, so much more carefree and graceful, when a slip doesn't necessarily mean sudden and certain death.

Now she's alone in a cluttered apartment, her only visitor the welfare nurse, whom she will not allow past her apartment door. Now she has Meals on Wheels—the truck had driven away two hours before. She had been putting off longer every day the disagreeable task of unlocking and opening her door to take in the tray outside on the hall floor, placed there most likely by the young one with the big hips. But they knew that the old woman would open the door eventually and take in the food. They could rest assured she would not die of starvation.

No, she will die by other means, by the rumbling and clatter of people living their collective lives outside the walls of her rooms, indifferent to her day after day and yet eager to see with their own eyes what that indifference wrought and to flay themselves with remorse. The tumult of their supplication was filtering through the locked door, the closed windows, the drawn drapes, assaulting her half-deaf ears, beating vainly against the dulled center within her. It was a searing grief to them, a holocaust composed of rejection and repentence, an exquisitely painful experience that they could describe to their friends and neighbors again and again for years to come. She was in mortal danger and knew it. She will burn like a martyr for them, feeling nothing.

They had been pulling down the old houses in back, houses that had been built when she was a girl. Then, of all the stupidity—and how stupid could they possibly be, in all that heat, with the yard out there like a tinder box?—they had been ripping shingles off the roof and throwing them down on a pile of burning trash.

She had seen them earlier that morning through a crack in the drapes—two men up at dawn, crawling around on the roof, ripping up with claw hammers the brittle, faded shingles, slivers flying in all directions, a performance without spectators, a curtain-raiser for her alone so that she might be wakened thoroughly for the main performance later in which she would have her role to play.

She knew by afternoon exactly what the spectacle would consist of. She had waited for it impassively in her Morris chair, her room already suffocating by that time with the oppressive summer heat, pressing its yellow eye against her closed drapes like a voyeur, daring her to open them up, morbidly inquisitive as everyone was to see what lay beyond them—what dust, what soiled laundry, what pointless mementoes, what scarred and pitiful furniture. And among it all a sagging old woman who kept herself shut away from everyone—a shriveled assemblage of obdurance and suspicion.

She had not always been this way. She could remember when anyone could approach her for comfort, for an afternoon or evening of pure enjoyment. She remembered, for instance, when one of her two sons had suffered some hurt, real or imaginary—and this continued until they were grown men, you must realize—how she was able to reach out and absorb that hurt so thoroughly in such a short time that they looked upon her as some type of miracle drug, always on tap. And when they finally left the nest, as all children must do eventually, she had transferred that same love and comfort to others, especially to Edward who basked in the extra attention and, when he arrived, to her grandson.

But then, when Edward died, when she could have used so thankfully some reciprocal healing, her sons, her grandson, they seemed to disappear. Had they left willingly or had she, as they maintained, driven them away? She had ransacked her memory in the face of this desertion and came up with no definite answer, and her heart had ached at first for abandoned mothers and for old women deliberately kept from their grandchildren.

She toted up the record of letters unanswered, gifts unacknowledged, visits canceled, like a witness in front of a trial lawyer. Pulling on her gloves with eyes cast down she asked the courtroom in general—Would it have hurt the boys to visit their mother once in a while, apartment-house bound as she had become? Would it have hurt the child so much just to see his grandmother once in a while? Was she so old and ugly? Her eyes stung with bitter tears.

Their father, traveling as much as he did, had never been close to his sons, so when he died she was determined to have them understand how it was with her and their father and how wonderful and loving, how kind he had been. She had tried to explain it to them, carefully, exhaustively. It had become so important they they understand completely. But it had been too much for them to cope with and they had stopped listening, had stopped visiting, had stopped calling her on the phone. Would it have hurt them so much to try to understand?

The fiery destruction continued to filter through the closed windows—two houses of her youth, side by side, the hip roofs once glowing warmly with new cedar shingles. Now they were old and ugly, gray and full of cracks, falling in ruins and no good to anyone, and part of a scene far away—sirens and shouting, heat and smoke—a scene in which she had some small part but which was of no particular significance in her life except as an intrusion, a harassment.

The room reverberated suddenly with breaking glass which fell in pieces onto the carpet and with pounding against the three locks on her apartment door. It had begun in earnest, she thought, the invasion. She put her hands on her knees and pushed herself up from the Morris chair, shuffled over toward the broken window, and stood behind the flapping drapes which she had drawn halfway open. She was wearing a faded and tattered blue robe. Her white hair was in tangles, her eyes empty, staring.

Over the sirens and shouts of the firemen, the people below were still screaming up at her—*Come down, come down!* Water and debris covered the sidewalks and street and the air was thick with smoke. The flames were licking over the roof above her while the crowd milled and pushed, straining their faces upward, barely held in check by a cordon of sweating, red-faced policemen.

She turned and looked at the ladder against the wall beside the window, partially obscured by the smoke which billowed and drifted everywhere. A steady stream of water was being played over the building and, looking down, she could see the head of a fireman bobbing from side to side as he labored up the ladder toward her. She backed away from the window as he reached the top, as he reached his hand through the broken window, his head dripping with water, his face blackened with smoke. She fumbled vaguely with her hair and pulled her robe closer around her and craned her neck past him to see the crowd on the opposite side of the street below.

Why was the fireman bothering? The old woman was determined above everything else not to leave her sanctuary of more than sixteen years. Intrusion, she thought. Harassment. The pounding at her door had finally stopped after someone in the hall had shouted that the roof would soon collapse. The smoke was stinging her eyes, but a tendril of peace took root and grew inside her. The fireman, on the other hand, was tearing and ripping at the window with a crowbar in order to enlarge the hole and climb into the room, in a perfect frenzy to carry her down the ladder bodily. She heard and saw it all, feeling serene and masterful, feeling—almost—triumphant. Indeed, it was not her problem, but theirs. She was quite aware that she was under siege, but knew also that they would never take her alive.

The crowd below groaned as though with one voice, as though the old woman behind the window had become to all of them a mother or grandmother or once-indulgent aunt that they had thoughtlessly left alone to fend for herself while they, unthinking, struggling so inexpertly to live in their own sometimes baffling worlds, forgot completely about her. Their hearts were torn with contrition for all the old women they had left utterly alone because of the ugliness of old age, for instance, or senility—an embarrassment to them before their friends, or for clandestine drinking of bourbon at breakfast, or querulous demands for custard and soft boiled eggs which were gummed moistly afterwards in toothless mouths. The people watching her from the street below longed to brave the deadly flames and smoke themselves in order to rescue that frail and staring symbol of their own shameful fastidiousness.

But the old woman would not expiate their sins for them. They had abandoned her. She was therefore absolved of responsibility toward them. A burst of water shook the apartment house walls as the fire licked closer and closer to the red-faced and dripping fireman, struggling to get into the window to save her. His face was contorted with frustration and fear. His eyes were starting out of his head. The old woman was staying maddeningly out of his reach and time was running out. He would not be able to reach her and take her out before the building gave way.

But what could she expect after he took her down there among the crowd but prying eyes eager to see her sore and wounded places, ready when the crisis was past to laugh behind their hands at her silly maunderings, her pathetic beliefs? Didn't the fireman know that? Didn't he realize that she would never step out of her window and back into the world with which she would be forced to make some sort of accomodation and in which she would be no more than a beggar? She knew this with blinding clarity: she knew that aside from expiation she was less than nothing to them, that she was of no particular use to anyone.

She had become so tiresome, you see. The boys had tried to explain it to her. The endless stream of memories had become so monotonous, the incessant calling up of their father, the inventories of trivial mementoes, the photograph albums scattered all over her rooms—it had all been so hard for them to cope with. Her face, moreover, had become ravaged and she no longer washed or combed her hair. The boys threw up their hands since they could do nothing for her and perhaps, they reasoned, were actually making things worse.

The apartment house roof began to rumble and crack ominously. The fireman wavered in the window and then, with heartfelt despair, left her to her fate, weeping openly as he hurried down the ladder toward the sidewalk.

The woman drew close to the broken window, smiling to herself, and squinted her eyes through the smoke to look searchingly at the crowd in the street below. Would it have hurt the boys to visit their mother?, she questioned them mutely. Would it have hurt the child? No, it would not have hurt them, but there you are. She turned her back to the window, groping and shuffling among the debris and smoke in the room, trying to locate her Morris chair. She found one of the arms just as the first burning splinters tumbled into the room around her. Then the roof collapsed with a prolonged roar.

The crowd surged back, straining their faces upward, trying to catch some glimpse of the old woman's body—perhaps hurtling toward the street among the chunks of brick wall and splintered, flaming wood. But she had of course been buried deep in the rubble.

Then after awhile the people left, trailing in couples and small groups back to their homes. And although they had been truly and deeply touched by what they had seen that day, their homes were not filled soon after, as we might have expected, by the mothers and aunts and grandmothers they had thought of so regretfully while they watched the plight of the lonely old woman.

But they did watch carefully the films of the fire shown on the five o'clock news, trying to find themselves among the crowd of onlookers. The prudent, after all, know what is best to remember and what is best to forget.

Joan Shaw was born in New Jersey and grew up there during the Depression; she has also lived in Maryland, Virginia and California. She was educated in California and Utah and has worked as a teacher and editor; she presently lives on a farm in Cache Valley, Utah, with her husband and children.

Joan Shaw began writing while an undergraduate and sold her first story to *Mademoiselle* in 1970. She has since published in other magazines and has been honored by the Utah Arts Council on several occasions. *The Uncle & Other Stories* is her first book.

*This
first edition of*
The Uncle & Other Stories
*printed for Cadmus Editions by
Mackintosh Typography in December of 1982
consists of a trade edition in wrappers and
fifty numbered copies bound in boards
signed by the author. Typeset in
Baskerville. Design
by Graham Mackintosh*

OHIO UNIVERSITY LIBRARY
Please return as soon as you
have finished in order to avoid a